Deadlock

Stephen Hudler

To my wife Amy,

Who loves this book even though she's not a sci-fi fan.

Love you.

CHAPTER ONE

E ddie Solomon frowned as the shutter on his camera flickered. Life as a private investigator was not what he wanted, but right now he was out of options. Surveillance on someone cheating an insurance company was a far cry from what he used to do. He thought back to when he worked as a

detective for the LAPD. Life was a lot better then, at least until three years ago, but he didn't want to relive that moment. The thought of it caused anxiety. If an attack came on, he'd be useless until his medicine kicked in. Just another headache to add to the list. He packed up his camera, ready to

put an end to another miserable day, when his brother called.

Great, I wonder what he wants now.

He sighed as he picked up the phone. "Hello, Lester."

"No need to sound like that," his brother replied. "Are you getting those pics to me today? The client's all over me to get proof of this guy doing things he shouldn't. And they want it sooner,

rather than later."

Eddie rolled his eyes and tried to keep the irritation out of his voice. "I have plenty of pictures that should make everyone happy, except, of course, Mr. Davis. I'll be at your office in about an hour."

"Don't be late. I'm calling them as soon as I hang up."

"Lester, have I ever been late a day in my life? No. I'm early for everything."

"Yes, yes. Bye."

Eddie's phone went dark. He started his car and made the trip back into the city to his brother's law office. It was a small practice, only him, but that's the way Lester liked it. He first started at a big law firm right out of college. Things went well for a while, but Lester was a type A personality. He didn't like following someone else's lead. He stole a few clients from that firm and began his own

law practice.

When Eddie quit the LAPD, he was adrift in a sea of pain and misery. He kept everything bottled up inside and refused to burden anyone else with it. When Lester reached out to him, it came as a surprise. Eddie always kept that part of his life separate from his life in Philly. Lester offered him to come home—an offer he didn't jump at right away. But after a few weeks, he realized Los Angeles held too many memories, the good and the bad. Eddie came home to Philly and took

the job as a private investigator for his brother's firm. It wasn't a glamorous job, but it paid the bills,

kept a roof over his head, and kept the dark thoughts of LA at bay... mostly.

He pulled up to Lester's office and put on his best fake smile.

Blair Benson greeted Eddie when he came into the office. She jumped up from behind her desk

and embraced him in a warm hug. She always made him feel appreciated.

She pulled back, grabbed his arms, and looked him in the eyes. "I'm so glad you're here. Lester's been pacing ever since he called you. I've tried to get him to calm down, but he just won't listen.

He's worried about this fraud case, you know. I hate seeing him like this."

Eddie gave her a look of sympathy. "I'll talk to him. I'll offer to buy dinner. That always puts him in a good mood."

He walked around Blair and into Lester's office. If there was one thing Eddie admired about his brother, it was his attention to detail. From the way he decorated his office down to his appearance. He always dressed like he was about to try a case in front of the Supreme Court. Tailored suits, polished shoes. His hair was receding, but he kept it short enough so it wasn't too noticeable. He even tried to get him to wear a suit. Eddie stood his ground—jeans and dress shirts. Lester

conceded, reluctantly.

"Les, I have the pictures. You can stop worrying," Eddie said. He tossed an envelope on the

desk and sat down.

Lester stopped pacing and straightened his jacket. He turned toward Eddie, his eyes cold and

flat. "Don't call me Les. You know I hate that."

"Yeah, well, I needed to get your focus off of brooding and on to other things. It worked,

didn't it?"

"Don't do it again." Lester glared at him once more before he lightened up and offered a smile.

"How'd the pics turn out?" He fanned through the envelope.

"There's no way Davis can get out of this. How long has he been defrauding the insurance

company?"

Lester sat down and tapped some keys on his laptop. "Almost two years. Every time they tried

to nail him, he'd admit himself to the hospital and claim another injury."

"Between the pictures and the doctor I found helping our Mr. Davis, he's done for."

Lester clapped his hands and stood up. "This is great news. To-morrow a representative from the company is coming, and we can begin our next move." Lester walked around his desk and put a

hand on his brother's shoulder. "Did I hear you say something about buying dinner?"

Eddie Solomon wasn't happy. But sometimes a little bit of happiness got through, and he felt

almost normal.

* * *

Fire trucks screamed by the restaurant, and Eddie snapped his head up. The mere sound of sirens was enough to cause an anxiety attack. They didn't happen often, but every now and then they

snuck in. Eddie's chest tightened, and it felt like his heart was about to be crushed.

Both Lester and Blair looked at each other.

"Where are your pills?" Lester asked.

Blair dug through Eddie's jacket, found the bottle, and fished out a pill for him. He swallowed it dry. Lester cringed. Eddie sat still, trying to control his breathing, and thought about his 'happy place.' He was desperate to maintain his composure. But he was just getting worse. His anxiety sometimes hijacked his common sense, and he let dark thoughts flood in and overwhelm him—like

the guilt. He felt guilty for letting himself feel happy, even for a moment.

He looked up and found Lester, Blair, and several other people watching him.

Eddie felt flush and excused himself from the table. He made his way to the men's room and splashed cold water on his face. How long would this plague him? He leaned over the sink and

gazed at his reflection.

* * *

"I'm going to check on Eddie," Lester said to Blair and then headed to the restroom. He found his brother staring into the mirror. "Blair's paying for dinner, and we're calling you a cab. You're in no shape to drive right now."

"I'm fine!" Eddie snapped. "I can get myself home!"

Lester didn't like being talked to like that. He knew Eddie could get defensive, yet he was here trying to help. That deserved a little civility. He fought back the urge to argue.

"I know you can," he said and put a hand on Eddie's shoulder. "You go home and take it easy. The insurance rep will be in tomorrow, and I'll be busy with paperwork the rest of the day. Stay home and rest."

Eddie looked over at Lester with red, bloodshot eyes. Then his face relaxed. He actually seemed relieved. "Thanks. I have a lot on my mind."

"I can tell. You have not been yourself tonight. You want to talk about it?"

"No, this is something I need to do myself." Eddie turned to leave. His shoulders were slumped, and he had a faraway look in his eyes. Lester put his arm around his brother as they walked out.

Blair was waiting for them by the door with Eddie's jacket. He took it, thanked Blair for her help, and gave her a peck on the cheek. She blushed and pushed a lock of her blonde hair behind her ear.

Lester took a friendly jab at Eddie's ribs. "You trying to steal my girl?" he said with a smile.

Eddie gave him a look and shook his head. "I'm not trying any-thing."

Lester shrugged and glanced at Blair.

"Well, you made me smile," she said.

The night air was muggy for May. Eddie carried his jacket and walked toward the waiting cab.

"Thanks for covering dinner, Blair. I owe you one."

Blair held out her arms to give him a hug. "Aw, don't even worry a—"

Out of nowhere, a blue beam of light tore through the sky and struck Eddie. Lester and Blair stumbled backward. It hit him on the top of his head and shot through to his feet. Eddie lifted almost a foot off the ground. The blue beam ran through him for almost a full minute, and Eddie looked like he was in terrible pain. In a pugilistic pose, his face contorted in a mask of twisted agony.

CHAPTER TWO

E ddie readied himself for another one of Blair's hugs when a sharp, stabbing pain pulsed through his head and everything went dark. A moment later, he opened his eyes and found himself standing in a large, dark room lit only by blue light flickering through the walls. It reminded him of the movie Tron but not so angular. The light moved through the walls like small bolts of lightning. He surveyed the room to see if there was any immediate threat. The room wasn't too hot or too cold. It had no distinct smell to it either.

He went to look around, but nothing happened. He couldn't move. He wondered if he had a stroke or seizure. He stood there for what he thought was an hour when two shadowy figures appeared. They seemed to float over to him and stopped a few feet away, keeping their appearance hidden. Eddie squinted his eyes. They almost looked like aliens—at least what everyone says aliens are supposed to look like—but something was off.

"We are the Eoch," said the figure on the right.

"You are our champion," the left figure said.

Eddie heard them clear as day, but their mouths didn't move. Did they even have mouths?

He couldn't tell. They spoke directly into his brain.

"What do you mean, champion? Where am I, and who are you?" Eddie demanded. He continued to struggle against his invisible restraints.

"We are the Eoch," the first figure said again.

And again, the other one said, "You are our champion."

Eddie's head spun with confusion. None of this made any sense. Aliens were something the tin foil hat guys believed in. They weren't really real. Maybe this was just a reaction to his medicine.

The two aliens started to make strange clicking noises, and Eddie heard this with his ears, not his mind, this time. The aliens began to vibrate. Small sparks of the same blue energy from the walls emitted off their hands. They vibrated even faster and fused into one.

The sole alien pointed at Eddie. "All will be revealed." Energy bolts erupted from its fingers and engulfed Eddie in an electric blue cocoon. His entire body tingled and vibrated like his captors.

No sooner had the beam hit him than he fell and hit the sidewalk. "Call 911," Blair shouted.

Lester ran over to him but stopped short. "You think he's electrified? Eddie! Are you all right?"

Eddie lay where he had fallen and took stock of how he felt. *I don't see any blood. I don't feel sore or burnt, and my shoes are still on.* He had seen the effects of lightning damage firsthand in Los Angeles when he was at the scene of an accident. A man tried to finish up a home improvement project just as a storm rushed through and *boom!*—second-degree burns on his neck and arm where he was hit, his shoes blown off as the lightning exited him. Unfortunately, the man didn't survive.

And while Eddie still wasn't sure what exactly happened to him, he knew he didn't want to go to the hospital. Wooziness pressed its way in.

* * *

The street became a beehive of activity. People pushed in to take pictures and videos of Eddie.

Lester heard sirens in the distance.

Eddie struggled to get to his feet. "Help me up. I'm not going to the hospital. I don't want

to be here when they show up," he said.

Lester went to his brother. He wanted to do the right thing, but he didn't want to get on his brother's bad side. He and Blair helped Eddie into his car, and they left the scene as fast as they

could.

Eddie was in and out of consciousness on the drive home. They maneuvered him through the living room into his bedroom. When they dropped him on the bed, he started to mumble. It was difficult to understand. It sounded like one side of a conversation. Blair turned off the light, and

they both walked back to the living room. Lester kicked off his shoes and sat down on the sofa.

"Aren't we going to do anything?" Blair asked.

"Nope. He wants to do things the hard way." Lester put his hands up. "He's never liked hospitals. I'm not about to have him wake up in one and realize I'm the guy who made that

decision."

Blair returned his look with one of concern. "If he wakes up at all."

* * *

Eddie's knees buckled. He braced himself for the fall, expecting a hard landing.

"What is this? Like some kind of spongy mat," he said.

He looked up, and no one was around. Instead of seeing the inside of his house, there was a vast expanse of space. This was not Earth's sky. It couldn't be. With a sickly green moon and countless spaceships firing on each other, this had to be a dream.

As he got back to his feet, one of the ships exploded, causing him to fall again. He brought his hands up to protect himself, but the debris passed through him as if he were a ghost. Eddie patted himself down and felt for any injuries or blood. But there was nothing. He got up again and found himself floating through the wreckage. Now he was sure this was a dream. No heat emanated from the fires around the downed ship. And it was eerily quiet. Eddie pulled at his ears, thinking they might be clogged.

"There's nothing wrong with you, human."

Eddie spun around to find a large blue ball floating in front of him. It flickered with electricity like the interior of the alien ship. He reached out to touch it, and a bolt flew off.

"Ow." He shook his hand, trying to lose the tingling sensation. "Well, something seems real here."

"You must have a lot of questions."

Before Eddie could answer, two tentacles grew out of it. They reached out and touched his head. Another shock went through him, and the vision of warring spaceships vanished. In its place was empty space—nothing but stars and swirling galaxies. Eddie's stomach churned at the sudden shift.

"What is going on?" he asked. He felt small electric shocks at his temples. The thought of this being a dream quickly faded. Now he was sure he was going mad.

"You are fine, human. You are not losing your mind."

"Then what's happening to me?" Eddie tried to reach up and remove the tentacles, but his arms were forced down to his sides.

"You have been chosen to fight for the glory of the Eoch Empire."

"Abducted is more like it."

"Call it what you will. You have been picked to act as the Eoch's champion. You should feel honored. With over seven billion humans on this planet, you were chosen."

Eddie attempted to move again, but his arms and legs were frozen. "So I was chosen," he said. "What does being the champion mean?"

The orb started to pulse. The energy coming off it increased and once again the view turned back to the battle he saw before.

"As far back as time itself, the Eoch and Thiar waged war. Two great empires wanting nothing more than to defeat the other and expand their reach. Over and over, one side would gain the advantage only to have the other match it and retake control. The war came to a standstill. The Eoch and the Thiar had become equal and nothing either side did could move the other."

Eddie watched as the fighting overhead played out along with the orb's narration. Ships of all sizes came in to sight only to be destroyed. *Countless lives lost. What a waste.*

"With the war being deadlocked, the two sides sent emissaries to discuss ways of breaking the stalemate. A solution was found. It was not accepted right away, but as both sides continued to lose resources and citizens, they came to an agreement. It was called the Omega Solution."

The scene adjusted again. Eddie still wasn't used to the sudden change of view. He thought about the wildest roller coaster he ever rode. This was infinitely worse. Planets and stars whizzed past him. It picked up in speed until everything was a blur of light. The scene stopped abruptly, and Eddie thought he was about to fly off into space. His body jerked and his knees felt like they would give out, but the orb kept him on his feet. Once he got over the change of scenery, he recognized the planet they stopped at. Earth.

"The Omega Solution called for both sides to search the universe for a planet far outside their borders. One that was underdeveloped and primitive. They didn't want to encounter any hostile aliens that might hinder their plans. This planet was selected."

"This planet is Earth. Are you saying that out of all the known universe, Earth is the most

primitive?"

The orb simply continued. "Once here, each side chose a being to be their champion. The process of choosing was not random. You were chosen not only for your sense of fairness but your deep, dark pathological scar."

Eddie laughed. "My wh—"

"You know exactly what we are referring to. There is a darkness in you. The Eoch feel this will give you a keen focus."

Eddie stopped smiling and took a deep breath. How could they know about that? He did everything he could to hide it from everyone. Even himself. Yet somehow the Eoch were able to drill down into his psyche and pull up the most secret parts of his soul.

The orb as usual did not elaborate. "And combatants are altered to give them an advantage."

"I thought you said they were deadlocked. How can they give anyone an advantage?"

"While the Eoch and Thiar are equal in battle, you humans are not. Your species possess a savage unpredictability that will aid in combat."

Eddie hung his mouth open in shock. Hearing that he was chosen because he was, in essence, a wild savage was more than he could handle. He struggled harder to free himself, but the orb increased the electricity. His head flung backward, and his jaw clenched up. The orb released its hold, and Eddie fell to his hands and knees. The ground still had a soft, spongy feel, and he was grateful for that.

"The champion who emerges victorious will determine which side finally wins the war. The Eoch and Thiar will have their armadas orbiting your world. The winner will open fire and eliminate the other. They will be eradicated from the universe, leaving the victor to return and claim the others empire for themselves."

"And what happens to us?" Eddie struggled to get to his feet. He stared at the orb as it bobbed up and down like a beach ball in a pool. "Well,"—he rolled his eyes as the orb stayed silent—"all that, and you have no answer?"

CHAPTER THREE

T he first thing David Shaw noticed about the motel room was the smell. The tangy odor caused him to shudder. He breathed deep, hoping to get used to it. He'd be staying a few nights and didn't want any distractions of any kind. The bed creaked as he sat down on it. He tossed his bag down and thumbed the four-digit lock. It clicked opened. Inside were the tools of his trade.

He looked over the knives and other sharp instruments. Each one in their own sheath. David never cared for guns. They were too noisy and didn't give him the up close and personal touch he liked. When he killed someone, he wanted to see the life drain from their eyes. He loved feeling their last breath on his cheek. After years of experimentation, he figured out the best way to take a life and never get caught.

He unpacked the knives, then laid out his clothes. What he wore was almost as important as the knife he used. He was careful to keep an unassuming look about him. Short, brown hair. He wasn't very tall either. He blended into society like human wallpaper. Being inconspicuous was an essential part of the job, but it didn't come naturally for him—or so his therapist told him.

He thought back to his time in therapy. After his dad caught him strangling a cat behind their house—and finding numerous shallow graves of other dead animals, he was admitted to the psych ward. At the time, David couldn't understand why he was there. They were just strays. No one would miss them. He felt no remorse. If anything, he got a surge of adrenaline from watching the
life leave them.

He remembered the diagnosis. Sociopath. So David played along, got released, and continued on his way. Unassuming, unremorseful.

He picked up his phone and checked his email. Instructions were supposed to be sent to him once he arrived in Flagstaff. He scrolled through the seemingly endless spam mail folder until he found what he was waiting for.

"Henry Peterson," he said. "Looks like I'll be paying you a visit."

* * *

The alarm went off. David rolled over and switched it off. The sun hung low in the sky. He pulled out a protein bar and bottle of water. David never ate at restaurants. The less people who saw him, the better. He looked over his assortment of knives and picked out a Ka-bar and a boning knife. He slid them into pockets sewn into his jacket, picked up a small bag with a change of clothes, and
walked out the door.

* * *

The address took him into a small development. Cookie cutter houses lined the street. It seemed the only thing to differentiate them from one another was the mailbox at the end of the driveway. David drove by his target's house. The car wasn't in the driveway. He drove out of the development and parked in a mall lot a mile away. He liked to walk—gave him time to visualize how he wanted the meeting to go.

As he walked up the sidewalk, he took notice of the neighborhood. No one was outside. Streetlights glowed, and everyone was probably eating dinner. David moved to the back of the target's house and picked the backdoor lock. When his job took him to someone's home, he always looked around. How people lived fascinated him.

Growing up, he and his father lived in a small two-room house with a garage. He hated that house— except the fence around the backyard, which kept David's "hobby" from being noticed.

Shortly after his 17th birthday, he decided to leave. He wasn't doing well in school, and his father never treated him the same after he was released from the hospital. David and his dad fought a lot. Most of the fights ended with a black eye—David's eye. He had a duffle bag packed when his dad

came home from work one day.

"Where do you think you're going?"

"I was going to leave you a note," he told his father.

"About what?" He dropped his lunch bag on his chair and walked into the kitchen.

"I'm leaving. There's nothing here I need or want. Besides, you never really wanted me

around."

His father turned and stomped over to him, his face inches away. "You're not going anywhere, you little piece of crap!" He poked David in the chest with every word. "You're not old enough or smart enough to make it on your own." He shoved him back a step or two. "You're so screwed up in the head, you'll be in prison before your next birthday, if you live that long." Another

shove, only this time harder. He continued to scream at him.

Something in David snapped. He saw his father yelling, but he heard nothing. Without

thinking, he balled up his fist and punched him in the face.

His father staggered back. Blood trickled from the corner of his mouth. He tried to throw a

hay maker, but David ducked under it, then ran toward him.

David moved behind his dad and punched him in the back of the head. "I'll live a lot longer

than you, old man."

His father stumbled and tried to steady himself, but he lost his balance. He fell face first onto the hardwood floor, causing his nose to explode in a bloody mess.

David moved in before his father could turn over. He kicked and stomped until there was no more movement. He went into the garage, grabbed the gas can they used for the mower, and emptied the contents onto the body and all around the room. When he got to the front door, he

took one last look at his dead father and then lit the room on fire without a single thought.

And he never looked back.

After David finished rummaging through the house, he sat down in a recliner and waited. He checked his phone for the time. His target was late. He started to wonder if something was wrong when he saw lights through the living room window. It was time to get to work. He remained in the recliner as Henry Peterson came through the door. He was carrying a bag of groceries in each arm.

He kick the door closed and used his elbow to turn on the lights.

"You kept me waiting," David said. "Grocery day? I have other things to do."

Henry dropped the bags of food and took a step back. "What? Who are you?" he asked in a

high-pitched voice. "What are you doing in my house? If you're here to rob me, I have—"

David stood up and raised his hand. "Rob you? That's insulting. You insult me. I wouldn't abase

myself with petty theft."

"Then why are—"

"Your employers are not happy with the course of action you plan on taking tomorrow, Henry." He walked around Henry as he spoke. "They're quite sure that the meeting you're going to have with the FBI will cause them unwanted scrutiny."

"I tried to talk to them," he said. "I showed them the data, but they buried it, so I'm going to do the right thing."

David slapped Henry. He didn't care what this fool had to say. He wasn't getting paid to listen to a sob story. "You bore me."

Henry cowered, but continued, "They're going to sell medicine that's dangerous to people, and the public has a right to know about it."

David raised his hand, and Henry flinched. David chuckled a little inside. "What they sell or don't sell is none of your business." The irritation came back into his voice. "You work for them, and they make the decisions."

"So why are you here? To talk me out of it, to scare me? Well, it won't work."

With an unseen quickness, David grabbed the back of the poor guy's neck and plunged the Kabar into his abdomen. He forced the blade in as far as he could, then stabbed him over and over and over. Twenty, thirty times? David lost count. He let Henry's bloody body drop to the floor. Now came the messy part.

David leaned over and cut out his tongue. Then he sliced Henry's gut wide open and disemboweled him. This would get the attention of anyone who thought about whistle blowing. Before he left, David went into the bathroom to change his clothes. He started to peel off his blood-soaked shirt when a shimmering light appeared around him. He looked around in confusion. He waved his hands in front of him, trying to swat it away to no avail. A tingling sensation crept in, first on his skin, then it penetrated him so fiercely that his entire body started to vibrate.

He tried to run but was frozen in place. Everything turned white for the briefest moment. As quickly as it began, it stopped—the lights, the vibration. And to David's surprise, he no longer stood

in the bathroom. He was in a gray room with what looked like an operating table in the middle.

Did I pass out? Am I dreaming?

He walked over and felt the table. Metal. Cold. An odd odor hung in the air, but he couldn't quite place it. A whooshing noise came from behind him, and he turned around.

Three figures moved on him with lightning fast speed. Before he knew it, he was strapped to the table. A light shone in his eyes. He squinted to try to see better, but it didn't help. He struggled

against his restraints until one of his captors spoke.

"We are the Thiar. You are our champion."

"Champion? What?" His anger rose, and he was more determined to escape his bonds. "You are going to be sorry when I get out of this." The threat failed to carry the kind of weight he hoped

it would. In fact, he sounded more like one of his victims just before he killed them.

"You will be remade. You will be our champion."

A sharp pain pierced his arm, followed by a cold sensation coursing through his veins. Then he felt nothing. He saw hands—or at least what looked like hands—put a knife to his chest. He thought he was being cut open but didn't feel any pain. Time stopped. He drifted in and out of a daze while his captors went about their work. When he was lucid, he heard clicks and chatter and thought that must be the alien's real language. When he was unconscious, he dreamed of alien space battles and

worlds he only saw in sci-fi movies.

Without warning, he was back in Henry Peterson's bathroom. He glanced down and realized something was different. He walked over to the mirror, but... *Wait, am I floating?* His feet lowered to the ground once he stopped moving. Who was this looking back at him?

He tried to remember if he had always looked like this. He leaned in toward the mirror when a sharp pain ripped through his head. Everything suddenly became clear. He leaned in, scrutinizing his new self and started to laugh. His voice now sounded like thousands of razor blades being dragged against a chalkboard. His

laughing shattered the mirror.

David Shaw was no more. In his place stood the champion of the Thiar, and there was no force on earth that could stop him.

CHAPTER FOUR

E ddie walked out of the bedroom, rubbing his head. He scanned the room. Lester lounged on his couch, and Blair was reading a book in his favorite chair. He felt dizzy and put his hand out to steady

himself, but it went straight through the wall. Lester and Blair both jumped up and ran over to him.

"How did I get here?" he asked. He pulled his hand out of the wall and looked at it. "And

what happened?"

Blair threw her arms around him. She took a step back with a bewildered look on her face.

"Hmm, you seem different."

"I do?"

"Come over here," Lester said. Eddie walked across the room.

"You're taller." Lester stood next to him. "I know you never let me forget I'm shorter than you,

but seriously, now you're even taller. Tell me your height."

"Come on," Eddie protested, "you know how tall I am. I'm six-foot-two."

Lester grabbed a tape measure from the junk draw and measured him. "This says you're six-
foot-seven inches."

Eddie shifted. *Something definitely isn't right.* "Hold on a sec."

He went to his room and closed the door. He stood in front of the full-length mirror, looking at himself, and shook his head. Things didn't make sense. He leaned in closer, thinking that might make a difference. It didn't. His clothing felt tight. He stretched his arms out, and the top few buttons on his shirt popped off. The stitching around the shoulders tore as well. *Really? I just bought these clothes.* Just then, he noticed the pain in his feet. He kicked off his shoes, and the pain disappeared.

He pulled off his shirt and pants and stood there in only his boxers. While he had always been in decent shape, the last few years took their toll on Eddie, and he let himself go. He had gained more weight than he was happy with, but looking at his reflection now, all signs of weight gain were gone. He looked incredible. Rock solid abs replaced his less than shapely middle. Muscles bulged from his arms and chest and made it look like he'd been lifting weights for years. Even his hair had
grown out. Eddie stared in amazement. A knock on his door made him jump.

"Is everything okay in there?" Lester asked.

Eddie rummaged around for some loose-fitting clothes. "Yeah, I think so," he said.

"Do you need any help?" Blair asked.

"No, I'm fine, thanks." He couldn't make out what Lester said, but Blair started to laugh.

"What? I'm just trying to be helpful," she said.

Eddie came out of his room in a t-shirt and shorts. They were still a bit tight. He moved over to the couch and slumped down on it. "I don't believe it. Whatever it was that hit me rewrote my DNA."

Lester and Blair stared at him like he was speaking gibberish.

"What do you mean 'rewrote your DNA'?" Blair asked.

"Look at me," Eddie said as he jumped off the couch. "I'm five inches taller, and I'm cut like an

Olympic weightlifter. It said they changed my DNA and choose me as their champion."

Lester shook his head. "Wait, who said they were going to use you as their champion? Are you sure you're all right? You got hit by a giant blue laser from space. I think maybe you should get

checked out."

"The Eoch. Good grief, you're clueless." Eddie threw up his hands and started to walk around the room. "And, Lester, I've told you repeatedly, no on hospitals. I'd have to fall into a coma or something before I ever step foot in one." He moved toward his brother. "Besides, look at me." He

raised his arms up in a bodybuilder pose. "I look better now than I did in my twenties."

"But why?" Lester asked. "What is happening to you? We brought you home, and you've been

asleep for almost two days."

Now Eddie looked confused. "Two days? Really?"

"Really," Blair said.

"We haven't left your place since the incident," Lester said. "The police showed up asking questions. Luckily, it was guys I knew—convinced them what was reported wasn't as bad as everyone made it out to be. I told them you were fine, but you might be coming down with the flu. I

don't know if they bought it, but they seemed satisfied."

Eddie sat down and told them about the dream. He told them about the aliens, the war, and their decision to use two beings from another world as champions. He watched the expressions on their faces as they took it all in. If Lester and Blair hadn't been there, they would've thought he was a loon. But seeing the laser and what Eddie looked like now, they couldn't deny something weird was happening. Things had changed, and he was afraid they would only get worse.

"So now what?" Blair asked. "This blue ball thing said you had powers. What powers do you have?"

"I don't know. They didn't tell me."

"Oh! Oh!" Blair pointed repeatedly at him. "This is just like that show, 'The Greatest American Hero.'"

"I loved that show," he said and smiled.

"I know, right?" Blair jumped over and sat next to him. "He got that suit that gave him powers, but he lost the instruction manual and had to learn everything on his own." Blair was a big fan of comic books and science fiction. "This is so exciting! Superpowers!"

"Well, I don't have a suit. I guess I'll have to figure out what I can do on my own too," Eddie said.

"We can help," she said.

Lester arched his eyebrow. "And how are we going to help?" "I don't know, but we can't just let him go through this alone."

"I'm with Lester on this one," Eddie said.

"Wow," Lester said. "We agree on something."

"Blair, thank you for wanting to help, but I don't know what you could do to help me."

Lester stood up, yawned, and stretched. "Listen, it's been a long couple of days for Blair and me. And I'm tired. I was able to postpone the meeting with the insurance rep telling him you were in an accident, but they're coming into the office tomorrow, and I need to get a good night's sleep."

Eddie walked them to the front door. "You two go ahead and drive safe. I'm starving. I'm going to eat and then figure out my next move. I'll talk to you guys later."

"I'm sure you have a lot of thinking to do," Lester said.

"You can say that." And Eddie closed the door.

* * *

Blair was exhausted. She opened the car door and fell in. Even though they had plenty of rest waiting for Eddie to regain consciousness, the emotional toll weighed heavy on them both. For two days, they stayed by his bedside. They argued about taking him to the hospital. Neither said much to each other on the drive to her apartment. But Blair didn't want the night to end with tension between them.

"You were right," she said.

"What?" Lester gave her a mixed look of confusion and irritation.

"I said you were right. Eddie woke up on his own." She hoped if she admitted she was wrong, it would ease the stress.

"He's always been resilient," Lester said with a hint of envy. "I've seen him take all kinds of abuse playing sports in school. Nothing ever stopped him."

"I know. But a... a laser from out of nowhere? That's not even a little normal. How do we know he won't relapse and never wake up?"

"For lack of a better word, Eddie's always been lucky," Lester said with a scoff. Blair wondered if maybe she should have stayed quiet. "Life came so easy to him. He never told me what happened to him in California, but it must have been bad. And bad things don't happen to the Eddie Solomon's of the world." Sarcasm joined his envy in an off-putting duet.

"You sound a little annoyed," she said, regretting the words as soon as they left her mouth.

"I had to grow up in a house with a brother who could do no wrong. And yeah, it pissed me off! He was dad's golden boy. After he came home from California, things seemed like they were getting better between us. Now he gets hit by some alien lightning beam, and he looks like a superhero. God only knows what else he can do now. Even when life dumps all over him, he comes out squeaky clean."

Blair's idea of easing tension seemed to have backfired. Hoping the car ride would end sooner than later, she gazed out her window. She never saw this side of Lester before—jealous and petty.

Maybe this tirade was just a by-product of exhaustion and worry.

Lester stopped the car outside of Blair's apartment. She reached for the door handle, and he grabbed her wrist—not in a gentle way. She turned and looked at him in shock. He let go and put his hands up in surrender.

"I'm sorry," he said. His hard, angry face on the drive over softened. "I've been a little preoccupied."

"I understand," she said and put her hand on his face. "You thought your brother might die. I get it." She looked into Lester's eyes—the bitterness was still there.

He shook his head. "It's not just that. It's everything. Listen, take tomorrow off. I'm meeting the guy from the insurance company, and we don't really have much else to do. I know I've been a little prickly lately."

"A little?" The amount of sass she used surprised her, but Lester didn't look fazed by it.

"Okay. A lot. I'm sorry. Rest up, and I'll be by tomorrow evening. We'll go out for dinner." "Okay."

They leaned in and kissed.

Blair got out and watched Lester drive away. She couldn't shake the feeling something still wasn't right with him. She hoped a hot shower and a good night's sleep would balance things out.

CHAPTER FIVE

David Shaw had a new purpose. Beings known as the Thiar chose him to find and eliminate a competitor. He thought about his mission and what he just became on the way to a motel outside of Flagstaff. He didn't know why, but he was drawn to it. The people at the motel ran in fear. Being feared pleased him.

He passed by several doors until something compelled him to stop. He pushed at the door, and it flew off its hinges. A suitcase and other items that once belonged to him were laid out on the bed. He didn't feel any connection to them. The person he woke up as this morning was dead. In his place stood what looked like the embodiment of death itself. The skin over his face was drained of color and drawn in. He wore a grayish outfit trimmed in red—a leather jacket and pants with military-style boots. A glowing red gem, the size of a baseball, was embedded into his chest. Red energy flowed through his body.

Nothing from his former life remained. Even when he tried to think back, nothing was there. No parents, no job, no name. He only felt one thing but couldn't place it. Was it something from his old life or something to do with his current one? The thought eluded him, but the feeling had a name—Zealot. He turned the word over and over in his head.

Harsh noises filled the air, and he floated to the window to investigate. Someone must have called the local police, because they headed straight toward his room. He guessed a levitating man that looked like the grim reaper was something someone would report to the police. He rubbed his

hands together, excited to try out his new body.

"John Smith, come out with your hands up," said a voice over a loudspeaker.

He lifted himself off the ground and floated out to the parking lot. Several police took cover behind their cars, guns drawn. His hands were up out of instinct, but he lowered them. He wanted

to see what powers the Thiar gave him.

"My name is not John Smith," his voice shrieked through the air. Everyone in proximity yelled in pain and covered their ears. He lifted himself into the air. When he was about ten or eleven feet off the ground, he continued, "My name is Zealot. You will not stop me from my mission." He let out a deafening shriek, and every window in the area shattered. The police dropped their guns and protected their ears from the noise. The force of the scream drove the police cars back. One even

exploded, killing the two officers taking cover behind it.

Zealot descended on the fallen police. His scream disoriented them, and they became easy prey.

He reached out and grabbed an officer by the throat. He lifted him up and looked him in the eyes. The officer's face filled with terror, and Zealot felt it. His face twisted into a grotesque smile. The police officer he was holding fought even harder to break free. Energy from Zealot moved through the officer, and he began to shake uncontrollably from his head to his feet. The gem in Zealot's chest pulsated and glowed brighter. The officer screamed in pain as electricity passed through him.

When Zealot finished, he threw the body down. It hit the ground—a smoldering husk.

The other police officers moved further back, but kept their guns trained on him. Zealot laughed when the entire assembled police force opened fire. He stretched out his hand and small bolts of energy intercepted the bullets. They dissolved leaving behind a cloud of smoke. He continued to float above the blockade. His smile turned into a frown as he stretched both arms toward the officers. Red energy leapt from his fingers. The attack lasted for only a few seconds, but

in that time every police officer was burnt beyond recognition.

Zealot flew off confident that no matter who the other champion was, they didn't stand a chance against his power.

* * *

The sun shone through Eddie's living room window, and he opened his eyes. He must have fallen asleep in his chair. After sleeping for two days, he was shocked that he still needed sleep. His stomach growled. He never ate the night before, so he headed into the kitchen and whipped up a hearty breakfast. After eating and figuring out his clothes situation, Eddie walked out to his car. He

forgot it was still at the restaurant... if the police didn't tow it already.

The restaurant was almost ten miles from his house. He decided to jog into town. Jogging helped clear his mind and think. He didn't feel any different, but as he jogged, he noticed that he was keeping up with traffic. He moved alongside a woman in a minivan and asked her to roll down

her window. She did but only a little.

"Excuse me," he said, "how fast are you going?" She looked down at her speedometer and then at Eddie. Her mouth dropped, and she held out four fingers, then five. Eddie was shocked. "Thank

you." He switched to a run and ran past her and all the other traffic.

Eddie's car was exactly where he parked it the night of the incident. He didn't go up to it right away because there were some people wandering around where he was hit by the beam. He wondered if they were some kind of sci-fi junkies looking for a souvenir of the incident. Eddie sighed. All he wanted was to get his car without making a scene, but it looked like that wasn't going

to happen. He walked up, and the crowd turned toward him.

"Hey, that's him!" They ran over and asked him question after question. Some pushed tablets and pens at him for an autograph. Eddie, as politely as he could, refused to answer or sign anything

and pushed his way through.

When he got to his car, he noticed several tickets under his wiper blade and a boot on his tire.

"Just great. That's all I need." He collected the tickets and chucked them in the backseat. The noise of the crowd surrounding him was maddening. He didn't know what his face looked like, but when

he turned to face them, everyone got quiet.

"All I want is to get my car and go home," he yelled. "Please stop bothering me." The crowd

backed off and eventually moved on. Eddie leaned down to inspect the boot on his tire.

"Why don't you try to break it?"

"Listen, I told you..." He turned and saw Blair standing there with a sheepish look on her face.

He smiled. "Break it, huh?"

"Yeah," she said. "I mean, I bet you could do it no problem." Eddie started to say something, but Blair waved her hands at him and cut him off. "Come on. You grow five inches and look like a

superhero. I bet you have super strength. Give it a try."

"All right. Stand back." He'd hate for her to get hit with any shrapnel. "Let's give this a shot." He turned back to his car and knelt. He grabbed the boot with his hands and, without much effort,

the metal snapped.

"Woohoo! I knew it!" Blair cheered.

Eddie suspected he might have super strength, and Blair's confidence made him feel good but also uneasy. Eddie didn't believe he deserved true happiness. Every time he got close to it, someone he loved got hurt, or worse. The happier he felt, the worse the universe would tax him to balance the cosmic scales, so to speak. Blair's faith in him sparked a tiny bit of happiness, and that bothered

him. No need to give the universe any ideas.

He glanced at Blair, then got into his car and tore off. He felt bad for ditching her like that but

kept driving. He had a lot on his mind and wanted to be alone to sort through it all.

* * *

Eddie parked his car and went inside to think about his next move. This whole superpower thing was a big deal. He didn't want to abuse the gifts he was given. Maybe he had other powers waiting to be discovered. A shower sounded good about now. When he was done, he dressed in yet

another baggy pair of shorts and a t-shirt. He went to the kitchen and found Lester waiting for him.

"What's your problem? What did you say to Blair?" He put his finger in Eddie's face.

"I don't know what you're talking about. I didn't say anything." Eddie knew exactly what Lester

was talking about, but he wasn't going to admit it.

"Blair thinks you're upset with her. She said you gave her a look like you were mad. You owe her an apology. Call her. Now." Eddie never saw Lester this mad before. Lester's face was flush, his

jaw clenched. This was a whole new level of anger.

Eddie backed up and put his hands up in surrender. "Listen. I don't know what's gotten into

Blair or why she thinks I'm mad at her, but that's about as far from the truth as you can get."

Lester wasn't satisfied with his answer, so he pressed Eddie like he was cross-examining a hostile witness. "Well then, what is the truth? What's the problem? When you got back to Philly, you said something happened to you in LA, but it wasn't something you wanted to talk about. I didn't press you about it. I thought if I gave you time, you'd eventually let me in on what caused you to

pack up and leave, but you've kept me at arm's length."

Eddie's anxiety roared back. He could feel his chest tighten and fought back tears. Lester deserved to know the truth, but Eddie was blinded with grief so strong he couldn't think straight. The memories of what happened three years ago swamped his defenses. Lester had him backed up

against the couch. Eddie reached back and lifted it over his head and screamed.

Lester stumbled backward and fell. He looked terrified and raised his hands to defend himself

although they both knew that was pointless. If Eddie wanted to hurt him, no one could stop him.

Eddie started to swing the couch but stopped as Lester put his hands up. Shame filled him. In a

flash, he saw the damage he could do to those around him if he let his emotions take over. He understood then that he couldn't keep a secret as dark as the one he carried to himself. He needed to leave and get his head together. The couch felt light, as if he was holding a pillow. He threw it through the back wall of his living room. He turned toward his brother—who looked like a deer in headlights—then ran off into the night.

CHAPTER SIX

Eddie was consumed with shame for how he treated Blair, not to mention almost crushing his brother. He also carried the weight of his secret around like a lead ball—the reason why he abandoned his life in California. If he was ever going to move on and get over the pain, he needed
to tell someone.

Eddie stopped next to a light post and sat down on the bench. He couldn't go back to his place with Lester there. After what just transpired, there was no way his brother would listen to
anything he said. And even with Blair upset, Eddie didn't have anyone else to talk to.

When he returned home three years ago, he tried to reconnect with old friends from his childhood. A few of them went out one night to a bar, and Eddie had one of his attacks. He went to the men's room to take his medication and regroup. But when he came out, his so-called friends were gone. "They thought you were mental and bounced," the bartender said. Eddie kept to himself
ever since.

Lester and Blair were the only people he let into his life, and now he'd gone and screwed that up. He needed to make things right with them, so he called Blair. She didn't answer. Not that he was surprised. He left a message telling her he was sorry and he needed to talk to her. She lived on the other side of town, but he was on foot. Then something from deep in Eddie's mind surfaced.

"I can fly," he blurted out just as a couple jogged past him. The man made a waving motion to the woman, signaling her to go faster. Eddie noticed the look he got. They probably thought he was some homicidal nut with the way he was talking to himself. Eddie realized then he wasn't quite dressed for the weather. Early May still gave some chill to the night air, and here he was in shorts

and a t-shirt. *Great, they think I'm crazy*. He could only imagine what went through their minds.

He could fly, or so something in his head told him as much. He shrugged. *Might as well give it a try.* He walked around in circles on the sidewalk and tried to reawaken the part of his brain that opened up and gave him the information about flying. He closed his eyes and imagined himself taking off into the air, the wind whipping past him. The view as he soared above the city would be awesome. He continued mumbling to himself, and a new revelation hit him. He knew what he had

to do.

Eddie opened his eyes and smiled. He was ready to fly. He checked to see if anyone was around or if any cars were driving by. It was bad enough there was a huge crowd at the restaurant when he was hit with the alien beam. He didn't want people pulling out their phones to video him in flight. The street was quiet. Whatever fed him the information about his powers 'told' him that all he had to do was focus his attention and jump. Eddie felt a little embarrassed but pushed that aside, looked

up, and jumped.

Suddenly, he was flying. He moved through the air like a missile, putting his fists out in front of him like superheroes did in the movies. This was great. He couldn't wait to tell Lester and Blair, then he remembered the way he left things with them. He vowed to make things right and flew toward Blair's apartment to talk to her about what was eating at him—the reason why he left the west coast and came east. He knew she wouldn't stay angry with him, but he'd been such an ass. He

hoped she'd listen to his story.

He noticed his vision was phenomenal. Even at night, he saw as easily as if it were daytime. Eddie knew there was more to his powers—there had to be—but he needed Lester and Blair's help if he was going to unlock them. It was time to put an end to his self-destructive path and stop pushing everyone he cared about away. He needed to get a handle on his life, his new powers, and

more importantly figure out who this other champion was and what he had to do to "win."

* * *

Blair flicked on the TV in her apartment. The news was going on about a man who killed nine police officers at a motel in Flagstaff, one with his bare hands. Eyewitnesses claimed it was a monster or demon. Others said crazy red lightning came out of his fingers and he hovered in the air. The

reporter stated the man fled the area and the investigation was ongoing.

Blair turned off the TV, and a wave of nausea swept over her. This was the guy Eddie needed to find—the other champion. She didn't want to think about it. Only true evil could do what he did to those people. And he might do the same to Eddie. She felt sick again, and it hit her so hard that she ran to the bathroom and threw up her dinner. After splashing some cold water on her face, she came back to her sofa and gently sat down. She couldn't handle any more drama today. Blair laid back to rest when someone started banging on her door. She jumped up, and her stomach churned

again.

It was Eddie. He didn't say anything but grabbed her up in a bear hug and carried her back

into her apartment.

"Easy, Eddie," she said. "I'm not feeling too good."

"Oh! Okay then." He eased her down. "Listen. I need to apologize. I was a jerk to you, and

you didn't deserve it."

"It's fine. All's forgiven." She walked back to the couch and sat down. "Look, it's kind of late. You know I don't mind you dropping by, but is that all you wanted?" Blair hoped he didn't come over to talk about the guy on the news. That was the last thing she wanted to discuss.

"No, it's not. I need to talk to someone. You and my brother are the only people I trust, and

this is something I've been carrying around since I came home."

Eddie's return to Philadelphia was a bit of a mystery. She thought about texting Lester to let

him know but then thought better of it. She gave her complete attention to her friend.

"Lester told me something bad happened to you in California, but he never said what it was."

"He didn't know," he said. "No one here knew. When I left Philly, I cut ties with everyone. I was determined to make it on my own and didn't want my dad or Lester to get in the way."

Blair paused. "Lester kept tabs on you. He knew you joined the LAPD and became a detective."

She hoped she didn't make Lester sound like a stalker.

"I knew he was. But there were parts of my life I was able to keep to myself. Things Lester or

my dad never knew."

She reached over and put a hand on his. "You can tell me anything. If you don't want Lester to

know, I'll keep it between us."

"I'll tell him later. He's probably still mad at me for swinging a couch at him."

Blair widened her eyes and jumped back a bit. "You swung a couch at your brother?"

He nodded sheepishly, and his face reddened. Eddie took her hands into his. "I've been keeping something from you two, and it's eating away at me. I was married." He must have seen the shock on her face, because he paused and swallowed hard. "Okay," he said and nodded, as if he was

psyching himself up.

He leaned back on the sofa and continued. "Her name was Emma. We met shortly after I got to LA. She was a nurse. A friend of mine on the force introduced us, and we hit it off. We dated for a

year, then I asked her to marry me."

"Oh, Eddie." She got misty-eyed.

"I told her how I was estranged from my family and I wasn't going to invite them to the wedding. She had a small family, and they all lived in the area, so we decided to elope and have a

small reception at her parents' house afterwards."

Tears formed in her eyes. "That's so romantic."

"Things were great between us. We were made for each other." Eddie stopped and looked away. He took a deep breath, then another. She could tell he was fending off his anxiety. Opening this wound had to be hard for him.

"It's okay. Take your time." She noticed tears were rolling down his face and he was shaking.

Blair put her arm around him. Eddie smiled at her, and his shaking seemed to ease.

"We wanted to have kids. Just after our fourth anniversary, Emma told me she was pregnant. I was happier than I'd ever been. Emma was eight months along, and she would get grumpy now and then. One day I was putting the crib together. She came in complaining about a headache and I was being too loud. We kind of argued, told her she was being dramatic. She really let loose on me then. I threw down the tools—had to get some air—and took off for a drive.

If I wasn't in the house, she could get some rest and get over her crankiness. I ended up running into some friends, and we had a few beers. Time got away from me, and I was there a lot longer than I planned on, so I said my goodbyes and headed home." As Eddie told his story, he had a faraway look in his eyes. Blair

suspected where he was going but hoped against hope she was wrong.

"My street was blocked off, fire trucks and police everywhere. I pulled my car over to talk to the officer directing traffic. I knew him from work. He pointed me toward the fire chief. Something wasn't right. I ran down the street, and my house was on fire. I ran toward it, but the chief and some of his men stopped me. My captain was there. He pulled me aside and sat me down. What he told me next killed me." Eddie's tears came faster. He took a deep breath and checked his pockets, but they came up empty.

"Do you need your medicine?" Blair asked.

He closed his eyes and composed himself. "By the time the fire department got there, the house was already engulfed in flames. My neighbor told them two guys went in to rescue Emma. They found her in the basement and got her out, but she was too far gone. They couldn't revive her. She died, and I wasn't there to protect her. The worst part... I left mad and never got to apologize." Eddie sobbed uncontrollably, and Blair cried right next to him. She felt helpless. All she could do was be there for him and help him through as best she could.

"I lost it," he continued through sobs. "I fell into a deep depression, and I quit my job. Life wasn't worth living. I sank into a dark despair I didn't think I was ever going to get out of. Someone from the LAPD found Lester's number and called him—told him I was in a bad way and thought he could help. Lester and I never had a great relationship. He didn't have to do what he did, but he

reached out and wanted to fix the rift between us. That's when I came home."

Blair wiped the tears from her face and looked at him. "You never told anyone what happened?

There are people who can help, you know. You didn't have to do this alone."

Eddie wiped his face on his shirt. "I know. I was proud, and old habits die hard. I had to figure it on my own terms. I saw a doctor about my anxiety and depression—once. She's the one who hooked me up with the medication. They tried to set up counseling appointments, but I canceled

every time. As long as I had my meds, I'd be okay."

"But going through a trauma like that you need to talk to someone. I'm surprised you lasted this long." Blair reached for a tissue and gave it to Eddie so he didn't have to use his shirt as a

handkerchief.

"That's why I'm here now. The medicine can only do so much, and this recent incident hasn't helped. I can't do this alone. I need a support system. You and Lester are the only two people in the world I trust. Will you help me?"

Blair leaned over and threw her arms around him.

Tears filled Eddie's eyes again, and he finally relaxed in her embrace. "This weight..." He

continued to cry.

"Let it go." Blair held him while he cried into her shoulder.

That's when Lester opened the door. "Um, should I come back later?"

"Lester," she said and waved him over to the sofa. He sat down, and Eddie reached out and hugged his brother. He returned the hug, his eyes full of questions.

Eddie pulled back and looked at him. "We have a lot to talk about." Eddie seemed calm as he told his brother everything. It was as if he held a renewed peace, something Blair was sure he hadn't felt for years. No one knew how to handle what was to come, but Eddie wasn't going in alone.

CHAPTER SEVEN

Z ealot peered out the window toward the barn and field just beyond. He didn't know how far he traveled, but to his luck he found an isolated farmhouse surrounded by acres of corn—just what he needed, someplace quiet. The husband and wife who owned the property never knew what hit them.

What was left of their smoldering bodies lay on the kitchen floor.

He moved to the living room and started pacing. Something bothered him. It felt like something trying to scratch its way out of his brain. He closed his eyes. It was familiar and foreign at the same time. He struggled to understand what was happening when he heard a voice in the room.

"I like the way you handled the cops."

A ghostly image stood in front of him—a man, perhaps, but its features were unclear. It glowed with the same intense red of his gem. Zealot took aim and his red lightning tore through the room, right into the ghost. It blew out one side of the living room, but the ghost stood there unharmed. Zealot flew at it but passed right through. Then he turned and fired up his lightning again, but it wasn't there.

"Settle down. I'm on your side," the ghost said. It reappeared behind him. Zealot lunged at it

again with the same result. "I'm not here. I'm there." It pointed to Zealot's head.

"How did you know what I was thinking?"

"I told you, I'm in your head. A small part of your mind the Thiar didn't wipe out."

"I don't believe you. This could be a trick by the other champion." Zealot didn't take his eyes

off the ghostly intruder.

"This isn't a trick." The ghost laughed. "You keep pacing like that, you'll wear a hole in the

floor."

"Why should I listen to you? What help can a figment of my imagination offer?"

"You've been thinking about how you could find this other guy and kill him. The Thiar turned you into a terminator." The ghost circled him. "You're focused on your mission, but you're going about it all wrong. You're trying to find the most direct route from here to him. Or her, we don't know yet." It stopped in front of Zealot and focused its hollow eyes on him. "Do something big to get this guy's attention. Call him out and set the terms. Have this 'champion' meet you where you

can have the upper hand."

"How do you, or I, know to do this? What were we before this?" Zealot asked.

"I can't answer that. I don't remember who we were or what we did. I can only remember we

were ruthless. And we were good at it."

"What do I call you?"

"You can call me Bruce."

"Okay, Bruce," Zealot said and nodded, "let's make a plan."

* * *

Blair and the guys drove out of the city and found a large open field. They wanted to test out Eddie's new abilities without any interference or unwanted attention. Eddie and his brother made their way to the field, while Blair grabbed a duffle bag with extra clothes, food, and water bottles. She meandered back and took in the view. The sun hung low. Blue sky with no clouds as far as she could see. Today was special. For her, this was a childhood dream. She read comics growing up and wondered what it would be like to be extraordinary. As the years went by, she picked up science fiction and fantasy novels. Sometimes she imagined herself as the hero. Other times she was the sidekick or damsel, and she was all right with that. Never in a million years did she think her dreams would become reality. Blair took a deep breath and released it slowly. She examined her

surroundings once more, then joined her boyfriend and the 'hero.'

Eddie jumped up and down a few times and touched his toes.

Lester just stared at him. "What are you doing?"

"Limbering up. I want to be nice and loose. I don't want to get a cramp."

Lester sighed and rolled his eyes. "I think you'll be fine. What do you want to do first?"

"Let's see how fast I am. I already know I'm strong, and I can test that easily at the gym later."

Eddie pointed to a dirt road off to their right. "I'll run a mile and see how long it takes."

Lester and Eddie walked out a mile. When they got back, Blair readied the stopwatch. He got

into a sprinter's stance and waited for the command.

"Go," Lester said, dropping his hand at the same time.

Eddie took off and kicked up a cloud of dust. Blair walked up next to Lester to ask him how long he thought he'd take. But before she could ask, Eddie ran up and stopped. Another dust cloud raised up. Blair waved away the dust and checked the timer.

"Incredible," she said. "You ran two miles in just over a minute. That's fast."

Eddie brushed the dirt off his legs and pointed at the timer. "Let's see how fast I can do flying." He went back to the makeshift starting line and with no prompting took off like a shot. The force of his take off caused a popping noise in their ears. No sooner had Eddie left than he was back.

"So how was that? I know it was faster than running."

Lester took the watch from Blair and checked the timer. "Just under ten seconds."

Blair ogled at Eddie. "Wow. You really are a superhero."

Lester sighed and reset the timer with a click. "Yeah, okay, what's next, guys?"

"I'll fly for a minute or so and land, and then I'll call you from where I'm at. That should give us a good idea of my speed."

"Sure. I'll just—"

Eddie took off leaving everyone's ears ringing. Their hearing started to come back to them when the phone rang. Lester gave his ear a few tugs, then answered the call.

"Hello? Okay, hold on. I'll call you back." He pulled up the map on his phone. "This is where he landed." He called Eddie back. "You're about thirteen and a half miles away. I'll—" He shoved the phone in his pocket. "He hung up on me."

"He did that in a minute?" she asked. The more the day went on the more Blair felt like she was living in one of her comic books. Seeing Eddie run and fly was amazing. Off in the distance, a shape came at them. "It's Eddie!"

He flew past them and into some bushes. Smoke came off of his shirt—a shirt, under closer inspection, that was in tatters. He smirked and pointed to the duffle. "I need a change of clothes. Apparently, a t-shirt and shorts aren't made to withstand extreme speeds." Blair ran over and grabbed the bag and threw it to Eddie. After a quick change, he came out and chugged one of the water bottles.

"So, is there anything else you can do besides fly and have super strength?" Lester's question

had a little too much sarcasm mixed into it.

"I can shoot energy beams from my hands. At least that's what the voice in my head told me."

Eddie raised his hands like he was about to box someone.

"You know that sounds crazy. You know that, right?"

"Lester, I just flew about twenty-seven miles in two minutes, and a voice in my head sounds

crazy?"

"Point taken."

"Let's see the lasers!" Blair bounced up and down like a kid in a candy store. She wanted to see

more. She couldn't get enough of the superpower stuff.

"What should I aim for?"

She pointed to a row of trees in the distance. "Try for that tree over there."

"Let's aim at something that won't start a forest fire. I have an idea. Be right back." Eddie flew off into the distance and out of sight. A few minutes later he came back with an old, beat up car. "I passed over a junkyard and saw some old cars in the back. This should be a good target." He took the car and slammed it into the ground front end first. "You two stand back. I have no idea how

much power this puts out."

They moved several feet back.

Eddie rubbed his hands together, balled them up into fists, and aimed them at the car. His hands started to glow, and then blue lights shot out and struck the target. The beams heated up the air like lightning and a loud thunderclap was produced just before impact. The energy beams were so

powerful the car evaporated without a sound.

"Did you see that?" Blair shouted. She punched Lester in the arm.

"Yes, Blair, we saw it." He rubbed his arm. "We should have brought ear plugs."

"What?" She gave Lester a smile and then threw her arms around him. This was the best day of

her life.

Lester just rolled his eyes.

"Okay, guys, while I could do this all day, I think we should wrap this up. It's getting late. So, let's summarize. I have superhuman strength, I can run and fly really fast, and shoot energy beams

that can disintegrate a car. That's everything I can do."

"And that's enough to take on this other champion?" Lester asked.

Eddie shrugged. "I hope so. Although, I'm not sure what constitutes a win. Let's not think about that now. Let's go home. I'll throw some burgers on the grill. We'll worry about tomorrow when it gets here."

CHAPTER EIGHT

Zealot didn't care why the Thiar gave him power. All he knew was that after he killed his competitor, he planned to use his power for whatever his heart desired. Bruce thought he should hire himself out to the highest bidder, make loads of cash, and live like a king. While Bruce went on about

money and power, Zealot focused on the plan to lure the other champion.

But Bruce was right about his mindset. Zealot thought too straight forward. He had no doubts about his ability to destroy the other, and his impulse to go directly at him was short sighted. "No plan is one hundred percent," Bruce told him. Crafting a strategy that utilized all their strengths

was important. They settled on a plan and launched it right away.

* * *

Mid-morning traffic in Reynolds, Nevada was at a crawl. A construction crew worked on repairing a busted water pipe, and cars were detoured around them. Some unlucky commuters waited ten to fifteen minutes for their turn to get through the mess. The driver in front saw the repair guys drop their equipment. They pointed at something in the sky.

"Hey!" yelled the driver. "Let's get back to work. Some of us have real jobs to get to." His taunts went unnoticed. The crew kept staring up toward the sky. The driver had enough and got out of his car to confront the workers. He made his way over to the one dressed the nicest, hoping he was in charge. Waiting in this mess costed him valuable time, and he wanted to make sure they knew it.

He paused and looked up to see what all the fuss was about. His jaw dropped as he watched a man flying in circles. He patted himself down, searching for his phone. No one would believe him without a picture or video. The driver ran toward his car but didn't make it. The flying man plummeted from the sky and landed right on him.

* * * * *

Zealot hit with such force it sounded like a bomb went off. Dust, debris, and bits of the unfortunate motorist flew up into the air. The work crew and those on the sidewalk were blown back from the impact. The windows of nearby cars and buildings shattered.

"Oops," Zealot said and laughed.

He walked out of the crater and into the middle of the intersection. With no warning, red lightning shot out of his hands and blew up a car trying to back up. The explosion caused even more chaos, and everyone ran for their lives.

This will bring us the attention we want, but let's turn it up a little, Bruce said from inside his mind.

Zealot smiled at that idea.

Some people rushed for cover in a building close to the intersection. He directed his earsplitting scream at them. They clamped their hands over their ears, but it didn't help. They fell to the ground, and blood oozed from their eyes and ears.

Lights and sirens caught Zealot's attention. The news stations weren't be far behind. Soon he would announce himself to the world and to his opponent. Police cars drove up from different directions, surrounding him. He flashed back to the cops at the motel. He killed them in seconds. It was instinct—the need to stay alive until his mission was complete. Ever since Bruce showed up, it's been fun, bordering on exhilarating. He looked forward to ending the lives of these people too. Adrenaline surged as Zealot let loose his lightning on the police cars. Two blew up even before they stopped. Other cars set up farther back, probably hoping to avoid a sudden death. A helicopter

came into view—a news copter.

This is our chance to call that other guy out, Bruce said.

"I am Zealot!" his voice boomed and blew out more windows. He heard people screaming in pain. "There is another like me. One with power." He turned straight toward the helicopter. "I demand you meet me, and we can see who the true champion is."

The news helicopter flew away, and another one took its place. Zealot could see it was a military

helicopter. It took aim and fired on Zealot.

"Base, this is chopper two. I've lost sight of the target. Wait I see—"

Zealot hovered off to the pilots left. His lightning ripped through the air. It hit the helicopter, causing it to pitch to the right. Lights and alarms went off as the pilot moved frantically to keep the chopper from crashing. His efforts were futile. A second dose of lightning blew the helicopter to pieces. Debris fell on an already destroyed downtown. A large portion of the helicopter hit a parked

car, and the explosion rocked the city.

Zealot gazed down at the carnage. A wave of euphoria swept over him, and he grinned. "Come

and find me, champion."

* * *

If one thing could get Eddie to unwind, it was grilling. After everything that happened to him, grilling helped ground him to normalcy. Just a man, some meat, and fire. It was exactly what he needed. He knew this was a small rest in a fight he didn't ask for. Things would get worse soon

enough, so a little break in the action was welcome.

Lester and Blair sat at the picnic table and nibbled on some carrot sticks, waiting for the main course of cheeseburgers and baked beans—Eddie's favorite thing to make. They traded stories about cook outs of their youth and the times when the fire got the best of the meat. After eating way

too much, they moved the party inside to the living room.

Eddie turned on the TV to find some sports to watch. It didn't matter to him what it was; he wanted it for background noise. The television came to life, and what they saw chilled them to the

bone.

News footage of a creature destroying a city in Nevada.

"That's the other champion! Ew, it's gross," Blair said.

It had what looked like a skull for a face. The white suit with red glowing tubes looked like something out of a science fiction movie. Eddie could make out a red glow in its chest. *That must be the source of his power.*

They stared at the screen. The amount of destruction it caused was incredible. First responders, firemen, and police worked to help the injured and keep the fires from spreading any further. The

news replayed the footage of it speaking to Eddie.

Eddie felt sick to his stomach. "This thing caused all this death and destruction to draw me out.

That voice is ear splitting. It's even got a super villain name and a suit to go with it."

Lester and Blair exchanged glances.

"You okay, Eddie? You're looking a little pale," Lester said.

"This is insane." Eddie got up and started to pace around the room. "Did it really call itself 'Zealot'?" He knew this would have to start sometime, but not this soon. And not this way. His
mind spun.

Blair reached out and took his hand as he passed her. "What are you going to do?" she asked.

Eddie looked down and saw tears in her eyes. Flying in a field and blowing stuff up was fun, but now things were getting real. Everything that happened to him in the last few days hit him, and he slumped on the couch next to Blair.

"What I have to do," he said. He squeezed her hand in reassurance. "You saw what it did to the police. I was given these powers to deal with that, so that's what I'll do." He hoped he sounded
confident enough to settle her fears.

"What about the military or the government?" Lester asked. "Couldn't they handle this?"

"I'm not sure they have a special agency to deal with alien threats."

Lester gave his brother a strange look. "This might be a bad time to mention this, but—"

"But what, Lester? Do you know something?" The intensity in Eddie's face stilled the room.

Lester swallowed hard. "Two guys claiming to be government agents came to my office looking
for you the other day."

"You're right. This is a bad time." Eddie got up and started pacing again.

"They had video of you getting hit by the beam," Lester continued. "I told them it was a hoax. I
was trying to protect you."

"I don't need your protection." Eddie raised his voice and pointed to the TV screen. "But those
people certainly needed mine."

Blair got up and moved in between the two brothers. "You need a plan," she said softly. "Come on, guys. We need to work together. You can't go off halfcocked, Eddie. If that creature thought this up to lure you out, then it's probably got something else for you."

Eddie dropped onto the couch again and put his hands over his face. His life was spiraling out of control. His head spun with all kinds of thoughts, most of which were not helpful. *Great*, he thought, *if this crazy freak doesn't get me, the anxiety will.*

"Right now, it doesn't know who you are or where you're at. Flying after him with no plan is suicide," Blair said.

"I know. Damn it! I feel so unprepared. I honestly don't know what to do." Throughout Eddie's life he always had a plan—even if no one else liked it. Today, seeing the carnage on television, he was at a loss. He had no idea how to approach, let alone defeat, this creature.

"Maybe we could call those agents for help," Lester said. He flashed a smile. "Yeah? What do you think?"

"You saw all the destruction it caused. I'm not getting anyone else involved in this mess." Eddie waved his hand, dismissing his brother's plan.

"But that's their job. It's what they do. They can help. Let them help you." Lester sounded almost panicked.

"No. It's my job. I was recruited for this." Eddie went to the kitchen. He grabbed a bottle of water out of the refrigerator and a bottle of pills from off the top of it. He tossed back a small, white pill and chased it with water. "Want one?" he joked. His anxiety was getting worse. He hated needing medicine to stay focused, but he refused to let his emotions overwhelm him. "For better or worse, I'm the one that has to stop it." He finished off the water and sat back down. Everyone was quiet for a while until Blair spoke up.

"So, I'll ask again. What's the plan? Zealot didn't give you an address to find him."

"I'll go to Nevada," Eddie said. "Good place as any to start. It might be waiting for me there."

"Or it might anticipate that and ambush you on the way there," Lester said. What a glass half

empty thing to say, but he had a point.

"No matter what I do, this is on me alone. You two, stay out of the way." Eddie got up and

motioned Lester and Blair toward the door.

"That's exactly what I was thinking," Lester said. He took Blair's hand and pulled her with him

out the door.

"Are you sure, Eddie?" she asked.

"You two go home," he said. "I have to get some things ready. Don't worry, I'll talk to you before I leave."

"But—" she started, but Lester wrapped his arms around his girlfriend and guided her to the

car door.

* * *

Blair ripped into Lester on the drive home. "How could you let him go by himself?" She

clenched her fist, and her nails dug into her skin.

"I don't know if you noticed or not, but we don't have superpowers. What could we do for him?"

"Moral support? Anything other than let him go off by himself."

"Moral support? Do you hear yourself? I really don't want to have this conversation with you now. Eddie is right. He has to do this alone. He's the one they chose." Lester seemed less concerned

about the situation and more annoyed.

She sighed. "I just can't imagine him facing that monster alone."

"Well, that's exactly what we're going to do. Tomorrow I'm calling those agents. We'll let them

do whatever it is they do in situations like this. Eddie can take it out on them if he wants to."

Blair didn't like this. Lester sounded like he didn't care what happened to Eddie. Tomorrow she'd go to Eddie and tell him why she should be allowed to help him. No one should have to face something like this alone. She was sure she could come up with a good enough reason. When Blair

Benson put her mind to something, it got done. And nothing, short of death, would stop her.

CHAPTER NINE

Eddie pulled the covers off his head and looked at the clock. It was 3:42 a.m. His anxiety went into overdrive ever since he watched Zealot's televised rampage. His prescription meds didn't even help. Maybe it was because of the sheer immensity of the act he faced. Or maybe his rewritten DNA just wasn't compatible with the medicine. Whatever the reason, his mind swirled with all manner of crazy thoughts. Why him? What was really going on? What is considered a 'win'? Sleep

eluded him, and he didn't think it would show itself anytime soon.

Eddie gave up trying to fall back asleep and made his way to the kitchen. He filled his coffee maker with water and measured out enough coffee for eight cups. He sat at his kitchen table and

rubbed his temples.

"This is crazy," he said to himself.

He thought back to when his life was more focused, when he had no doubts about his own actions. He wanted this to be a dream. Something he could wake from and tell his friends about the next day. But that wasn't going to happen. He never thought he'd end up where he was, not in a million years. So far away from the life he had. He grabbed his coffee mug from the cupboard and

poured himself a cup. He sat back down at the table and continued to think out loud.

"What am I going to do? How am I supposed to stop that monster?" Eddie looked up. "Did you know this would happen when you picked me? Did you know the kind of guy you were putting

your faith in? I don't think you did." He laughed. He imagined the aliens at the table looking back

and forth at each other and shrugging their shoulders—if they had shoulders.

Eddie understood pressure. Living in Los Angeles as a cop, then a detective, pressure was not a new concept. But this was something else. The weight of not just his life, but the lives of the people he cared about. If he lost, what would this monster do? How much damage could he cause? He knew the Eoch wanted him to be their champion, but he needed to think about his own world too. When this is all over, they'll leave and we'll be the ones to clean up the mess. And if Zealot wins,

then no one will be safe.

Eddie poured a second cup and walked into the living room. He stared at the plywood covering up the hole in his wall. He started to think of excuses he'd give the contractor when he

showed up to fix it, if he was still alive then.

He looked up and yelled, "What is a win?" He didn't know if they could hear him, but he yelled anyway. "What do I have to do to win? If I pin him, does a ref give us a three count and declare me the victor? Do I make him say uncle?" In his heart, he already knew the answer, but he didn't want to admit it out loud. In all his time with the LAPD, he never took a life. He pulled his gun. A lot. He

even shot a few guys but never fatally.

He drifted back to a time when he was only a year or so on the force. He and his partner, Harris, were called to an armed robbery. The perp had held up a liquor store and ran off on foot. Before long they caught up with him and hit the lights and siren. The guy ducked around a corner. Eddie

and Harris pulled their guns and took cover behind the car.

"Throw out the gun and come out with your hands over your head," Harris yelled. The guy swung around the corner and started shooting. Eddie froze. He trained and drilled so at a time like this, his instincts would kick in and he'd do what he had to without thinking.

Harris shot twice and took the guy down. He walked over to the crook, kicked his gun away,

and checked his pulse. "He's dead."

Eddie, still a bit frozen, holstered his gun and walked over to Harris.

"What happened?" he asked Eddie.

"I don't know. I... I don't know." His face reddened. Somewhere deep inside, he was afraid of

pulling the trigger. He felt embarrassed and ashamed.

"If you had been alone, he could have killed you. You can't be indecisive in situations like this."

Harris went back to the car and called for an ambulance and backup to help secure the scene. From that time on, Eddie never hesitated. He made sure he was going home alive at the end of

every day. Newly married, he wasn't about to make his wife a widow.

But his hesitation came back now. Just a few days ago, he was an ordinary guy trying to make it from one day to the next after an unimaginable tragedy. Then out of nowhere he became the champion of some alien civilization, tasked to stop a homicidal super villain maniac. Nothing in his

life prepared him for this.

He turned on the TV and the news was still reporting on the attack. The live feed showed soldiers and police scouring the area. Men in dark suits moved in and out of the scene. They had to be with the agency that talked to Lester. Everyone heard the stories of guys dressed in black

investigating UFO sightings. Looks like the stories were real.

The camera caught a man picking through the debris in the crater Zealot made. The police moved in to escort him from the area. Eddie could just make out his pleas for help. The man was looking for his wife. He looked completely and utterly broken as the police moved him away. Eddie identified with that man's pain. Seeing the devastation, he doubted there were any survivors. He clicked off the television and sat up a little taller on his couch. In that moment, something came alive in him—a sense of duty. Even though he wasn't a cop anymore, he still had an obligation. He took an oath to protect and serve, and Eddie was the only one who could stand up to that monster.

He'd be damned if he let Zealot destroy another city.

CHAPTER TEN

The combination of the sun shining through her window and the phone ringing caused Blair to wake from her deep slumber. She threw the blankets off and almost fell out of bed. She didn't sleep well the previous night. She worried all night about Lester and his outburst concerning his brother. The history of animosity between them was no secret to her, but she thought the two were getting along. Obviously not, at least not on Lester's side. He seemed off ever since the alien beam incident. She tried calling him last night after he dropped her off. He didn't answer. She felt like he was pulling away.

This was not the Lester Solomon she grew to love. On the other side, she worried about Eddie.

The destruction of the town in Nevada was heartbreaking to watch. Hearing that thing challenge Eddie was even worse. The two men that meant the most to her were dealing with matters she couldn't begin to fathom. Blair was an only child and had loving parents. She had a hard time understanding Lester's resentment toward his brother. Eddie's problem was even harder to wrap her head around. There was nothing in her life that she could use to comfort him.

Strange beams of light from space, changes in appearance, alien-looking creatures looking for a fight. These things were way over her head. Nonetheless, she was determined to stand by both men

in their time of need.

She grabbed her phone off the dresser. The light blinked. Lester had left a voice message.

"Blair, it's me. I'm sorry about last night. Let's get some lunch today. Come over to my place,

and we'll call out for Chinese. Love you."

A small wave of relief passed over her. She wanted to talk to him more about his anger toward his brother. She clicked the button on her phone, and the clock came up, 8:33 a.m. *I need a shower and coffee.*

After she drank her second cup of coffee and finished getting ready, she called Lester. His phone went straight to voicemail. She hung up without leaving a message. Blair figured anything she

wanted to say to him could wait until she was at his apartment.

On the drive over, she turned on the radio. "Cleanup continues in Reynolds, Nevada. The community is pulling together to help aid in the aftermath of the vicious and deadly attack. The confirmed number of dead is at seventeen. No new information has been given about the attacker

or his strange demands."

Blair shut the radio off and shuddered. The world, as she knew it, was now stranger and more

dangerous—a combination that made her uneasy.

Blair thought about the apology Lester left. *He's been distracted lately.* With everything going on,

she hoped a nice meal, and other things, might lighten his mood. But deep down she knew better. Lester doesn't let go once he gets a hold of something. And the bitterness he held toward his

brother wasn't going away any time soon.

Blair arrived at Lester's apartment and went inside. The food had already been delivered and

Lester was plating it.

"Just in time," he said. The smile he gave her was fake. It was the same one he used with clients he didn't care for.

"Are you all right?" she asked.

"I'm fine. Never better." The smile slipped and became a grimace. Blair cocked her head and

his smile, or what he passed off as one, came back.

"Lester, I know you've been out of sorts lately." She went over to him, took the plates out of

his hands, and led him over to the sofa. "I have an idea to fix it."

"Okay, let's hear it." His faux smile disappeared, and he became serious.

"We both love Eddie," she started.

He got up and moved away from her. "Why is it every time we get together, you feel the need

to bring up Eddie?" He threw his hands up. "I know what's going on."

"What's going on?" She folded her arms. *Why is he acting this way?*

He turned his back to her. "You want to be with him now, don't you?"

"Where is this coming from? I never thought about him like that. If anything, he's like the big

brother I've always wanted." Blair felt tears roll down her cheeks.

"I'd like to tell you a little story." Lester spun around, zipped across the room, and sat down next to her. "When we were teenagers, I had a girlfriend. I wasn't as popular as my brother, so the

girls didn't notice me. But one did."

Blair backed away a little. The look on his face worried her.

"Her name was Rachel. I thought we were going to be together forever. She was meeting me at my house after school so we could work on a project. Of course, I ran late." Lester turned his head

with a faraway look in his eyes.

"I was only a half an hour late, but that's all it took. I caught them in bed making out. She didn't seem to notice that she lost her top. Or me!" He slammed his fist on the back of the sofa. "We had never done anything like that, and we'd been dating for four months. But what Eddie Solomon wants, he gets."

"You were just kids back then," she said. "Kids do stupid things." She shifted uneasily. "And anyway, it's not like that with us. I want to work through Eddie's problems as a family. He needs

both of us." She reached out to take Lester's hands, but he pulled away, crossing his arms.

"He has everything he needs," he said with disgust. "He's always gotten everything he's wanted." Lester got up and looked up at the ceiling. He pointed at something Blair couldn't see. "Now, thanks to some alien light show, he's got even more. Power that men only dream of. It's natural for you to want to be with him."

Blair got to her feet and went to Lester. She put her arms around him and held him tight. "You're all I want," she whispered in his ear. He pushed her away. Her mouth quivered, eyes

glistening with tears.

"You need to choose," he said.

"Choose? Why?" Her heart broke, seeing Lester act this way. As far as she knew, she never gave

him any reason to question her loyalty.

"If you want to help Eddie, then go. Or you can stay here with me, and he can fight that thing

on his own, like he's supposed to."

Blair, still crying, picked up her purse and made one last plea. "Please, Lester, you don't have to

make this so black and white. We can be together and support Eddie."

Lester walked over to the containers of food and swept them into the garbage. Then with no emotion, he pushed past her and into his bedroom, slamming the door behind him.

Blair burst out of the front door, not bothering to close it. She ran down the single flight of stairs and into her car where she sat and continued to cry. People walked past and stared, but she didn't care. She pulled herself together and drove away not knowing if she'd ever see Lester again.

CHAPTER ELEVEN

L ester wasn't answering his phone. Eddie tried five times already, each time met by voicemail. He put his phone down and continued his research, pouring over any video of Zealot
he could find.

There was some video from a bystander in Arizona. It was shaky and difficult to make anything out. But the sound of the lightning crackling mixed with the screams of the police was enough to keep any sane person from sleeping for weeks. The video from Nevada was a

different story. He wanted to be seen. He wanted Eddie to know he was ready for him.

Eddie scoured every second of the video—even went as far as to buy a video editing program online. He slowed it down to locate any weaknesses, any chink in Zealot's armor. Zealot's apparent hatred of human life made him extremely dangerous. Nothing would get in his way—no person, either. Eddie still wasn't sure what counted as a win, but he was beginning

to think that it meant death. *Hopefully not mine.*

Eddie was so focused on the task before him, he almost didn't spot the movement in the room out of the corner of his eye. He jumped up and, without a thought, let an energy bolt fly

out of his fist. The bolt landed just in front of the intruder.

Blair screamed and stumbled backward. With his quick reflexes, Eddie rushed over and caught her before she hit the floor. He picked her up and brushed off the splinters of wall that

had exploded around her.

"Jeez, Blair, I could have killed you!"

"I'm sorry. I don't have anyone else here to turn to. You and Lester are the only ones I have." Her eyes were red and puffy, makeup streaked down her face. "And now I might lose him. He thinks I want to leave him for you."

"That's ridiculous. How could he think something like that?"

"He's jealous of you," she said. "He blames you for everything that went wrong in his life. He says you were handed whatever you wanted and took the rest." Blair convulsed and started to cry again. Eddie led her over to the couch. He handed her a box of tissues and sat down next

to her. She wiped her eyes and face.

"Lester knows that's not true. I worked hard for what I got," Eddie said.

Blair composed herself and continued. "He told a story about his high school girlfriend. Apparently, you stole her away from him—caught you and her... together." She made a hand

gesture to help explain what she meant. "Does he mean Rachel?" he asked.

She nodded.

"He knows that's not what happened." Eddie paced around the room. "She came to me and said she caught Lester with another girl. She wrapped her arms around me and started to cry. Being teenagers, one thing led to another. As soon as I found out she lied to me, I broke it off. It was a crappy thing to do to someone, especially when it's my brother."

"And Lester's been harboring even more anger toward you ever since you were hit with that beam."

"I never wanted any of this," Eddie said and put his face in his hands. "My life was screwed

up enough without getting caught up in some crazy alien war. I'd give it away if I could."

"Well, whether he has a reason or not, he's mad at both of us," she said.

"I've been trying to call him all day. It just keeps going to his voicemail."

"Now you know why."

He shook his head. This was not the time for Lester to start dragging out old high school drama. Zealot was the priority now. He didn't want any more blood on his hands because of some alien psycho trying to get his attention. Eddie went to the kitchen and grabbed waters for

himself and Blair, then popped two more anxiety pills. *Probably won't help, but can't hurt, right?*

Blair walked over to the computer and examined the still frame. It was frozen at a spot

where Zealot was shooting lightning into a building. His expression looked like one of joy.

"He's an ugly piece of work," she said.

"Yes, he is. Now, if only I could find something to use against him."

"We can talk about it on the road."

"We? There is no 'we.' I have to do this on my own," he said. "I'm not having you come

along and get in the way."

"I won't." Blair laced her hands together like she was praying and smiled. "I'll stay out of your way when things hit the fan." Eddie knew of her comic book obsession. He was sure she wanted this more than anything—to live out a childhood fantasy and watch a superhero-villain battle. She'd be in heaven. He liked them as a kid too, but this was real life. He didn't want her

anywhere near him and Zealot when the fight finally broke out.

"Please," she begged, "I can help. I can do whatever you need. I want to be part of this." This was out of character. In the three years since he met her, Blair never pushed herself into dangerous, or even slightly risky, situations.

"I'm sorry. I have to put my foot down." Eddie actually put his foot down, and it broke through the floor. He pulled it back with some surprise. "This is going to be too dangerous.

What would you do if the unthinkable happened and I lost?"

"I never thought of that. Then again I never imagined you losing." Her smile never faded.

She tilted her head and batted her blue eyes at him.

Eddie let out a laugh. How long had it been since he'd done that? Eddie came to love Blair like a sister. He wasn't about to risk her life. He lost too much already. "If you won't go on your

own, then I'll have to take you home myself."

"I'll find you and follow you," she said. "You need to have someone with you. Please. You shouldn't do this yourself." Eddie gave her a stern, almost fatherly, look. Her smile disappeared.

She sighed and walked back to the couch. "You're right. I don't want you distracted."

"I'm glad you understand." He hated to treat her like a child, but if that's what it took to

keep her out of trouble, then so be it.

"Promise you'll call me when it's over," she said.

"With the way this guy operates, it'll be all over the news. But yes, I'll call you when it's

over."

Blair jumped up and hugged Eddie tight around the neck.

He continued, "Besides, you need to talk to Lester and work things out. He needs you right now more than I need you." Eddie lifted her up so they were looking eye to eye. "You are the two most important people in my life, and I want things back to the way they were. More or

less." He gave Blair a kiss on the cheek and set her down.

She smiled and nodded.

"I have to get back to studying this monster. Go home and get some rest." He walked her

to the door.

As soon as he opened the door, a unit of men in black military outfits rushed in. They brandished weapons Eddie had never seen before in his life, all trained on him and Blair. He took on a fighter's stance and stood in front of Blair. In all, there were twenty armed men in his house and even more outside. From out his window, he could see an SUV and a large black panel truck. Two men in suits followed the soldiers in.

"Mr. Solomon, we'd like you to come with us."

"And you are?" Eddie leaned in, waiting for a response.

"I'm Agent Smith, and this is my partner, Agent Jones." "Yeah, sure you are," Blair said as she peaked around Eddie.

Two soldiers approached them.

"I'm not going anywhere with you," Eddie yelled. The force of his voice pushed back a few

of the soldiers directly in front of him. They readjusted themselves and took aim again.

"We are aware that you can easily defeat us," Jones said. "But if you try anything, we'll

defend ourselves. And we can't be sure what will happen to Ms. Benson in the cross fire."

Eddie eased his posture and raised his hands. "Fine. You win. I'll come with you. Blair was

just leaving."

"She'll be coming with us too." Smith reached out to grab her by the wrist. She pulled her

arm away and stepped back against Eddie. "This is non-negotiable, Mr. Solomon."

"I swear, if anything happens to her, I'll—"

Jones raised his hand to cut him off. He put his other hand to his ear as if listening to

something. "Yes, ma'am. We have them both... We're on our way."

They were led out of the house and into the SUV. While Jones hopped into the truck with the rest of the team, Smith entered the driver's side of the SUV. There was a soldier in the passenger's seat. Two more soldiers sat behind Eddie and Blair. As soon as the engine turned over, all the windows faded to black. Eddie and Blair looked at each other with puzzled

expressions.

"How do you expect to drive with a blacked-out window?" Eddie asked.

"I'm not driving," Smith said.

And with that, the SUV started to move on its own.

* * *

They had no idea how long they had drove for or in what direction, but the car finally stopped and the windows became clear again. The doors opened by themselves. Smith and the

soldiers exited. Eddie swung around to get out, and Blair grabbed him.

"What are you doing?" she asked. "We don't know what's out there."

"It'll be fine," Eddie said. "Just stay beside me." They exited the vehicle and found themselves surrounded by a huge wooded area. A dirt path led toward what looked like a small

bunker. Eddie looked over at the agents. "There's no way we're all fitting in that."

"Don't worry. It's bigger on the inside," Smith said.

CHAPTER
TWELVE

The metal door slammed shut behind them. It sounded like being locked in a bank vault. The agent was right about it being bigger. The hallway sloped down and broke off into several other hallways, kind of like a spider web. Old steel pipes along the ceiling and hallway walls made the place

look old.

"You could use some updated lighting. When was this installed? The turn of the century?"

Eddie hoped to get some kind of information out of them, but their chaperons were tight-lipped.

Blair seemed calmer than Eddie would've guessed. She never experienced a situation like the one before them, then again neither had he. Dark-suited government types with secret bases were

supposed to be a sci-fi trope used in comic books and movies.

"Any idea when this forced march is going to be over?" Eddie asked. He leaned over toward

Blair so he could whisper. "How you holding up?"

She had her arms crossed. She looked up at him, biting her lip. Her eyes were wet like she was

holding back tears. "I should have listened to you."

"Don't worry. We'll get through this."

"The way I left things with Lester—"

"He was the one who went drama queen, not you."

"But..." She was losing her fight to keep the tears at bay.

"You will see him again. I promise."

One of the agents turned and put a finger over his lips to hush them. Eddie returned the gesture

by drawing his fingers across his mouth, signifying he'd 'zip it.'

The agents turned them down a corridor that was much brighter than the rest of the place. The

carpet and the walls were all white. It led to a door with the letters "HR" emblazoned on it.

"Oh, we're going to human resources. Good. I want to file a complaint." Eddie grinned.

Their escorts remained quiet and stone-faced. Agents Smith and Jones nodded and the other

agents turned and walked away. Smith opened the door and motioned for them to come inside.

"Mr. Solomon, I am very excited to meet you." From behind the large desk at the far side of the room came a short, round older woman. She wore the same black suit as everyone else, her silver hair up in a bun. He noticed she had a slight limp as she made her way over. She put

her hand out and shook Eddie's. "You've got quite a grip."

"Thanks. I work out." He was surprised his anxiety hadn't kicked in yet. He didn't know

why, but he was thankful. He needed a clear head.

"Mr. Solomon, my name is HR. I'm the head of Cloak and Dagger."

"HR? That's... different." Eddie's detective skills kicked in. Who was she, really? HR isn't a name. Is it a randomly assigned title, or does it have a deeper meaning? He watched her as she moved around to her desk. He guessed her age at mid to late fifties, height about five-foot-three. While a bit overweight, she carried it well.

Everyone around her did what she said without question, which meant she was either well respected or feared. Eddie turned all this and more

over in his head as she continued to talk.

"Please sit. We need your help. And I think we could help you out as well."

"Really?" He crossed his arms and leaned back in his chair.

"Mr. Solomon, we know about your 'abilities.' We've had our eye on you ever since your little lightening incident." HR pushed a button on her desk. A screen came to life behind her

with a video of him suspended in the air by the beam.

"Eddie, I didn't know people recorded you," Blair whispered.

"Of course they did. It's the world we live in," he said. He put his hand on Blair's and gave it a squeeze.

"I assume you've seen the news lately?" HR continued. "Some superpowered nut is blowing up cops and cities to get the attention of someone he calls a champion. We know that

person is you."

"And you know this how?"

"Cloak and Dagger monitors and, when necessary, contains alien threats. Finding you was

child's play."

"Then let me go so I can find this guy and put an end to it." Eddie's cool exterior started to

crack. He could feel a slight tightness in his chest. He took a deep breath and let it out.

"It's not that easy." HR leaned forward, making eye contact with him. "We have questions.

For both of you."

"Questions?" he asked. "You just said you've been watching me. Seems to me you know

enough."

"Specifics. How long after you were hit with the beam did you develop your abilities? What

can you do? Do you have any weaknesses? Things like that."

"I slept for two days after the beam hit me. In that time I was told—in a dream—that two alien forces came to Earth. The Eoch and Thiar. They each chose someone to act as their champion. When I woke up, I was like this." Eddie stood up with his arms in the air. He turned around in a circle, presenting himself to HR, then sat down again. "As for weaknesses, I have a

hard time passing up a good piece of pumpkin pie." He flashed a grin and a wink.

"Mr. Solomon, despite the way we picked you up and brought you here, we are on your

side. We want the same thing."

Blair rolled her eyes and let out a little laugh. "Secret government organization pledged to protect the Earth?" Eddie was surprised by her sarcasm.

"Yes. That's exactly who we are," HR said. "We've been at it for over 100 years. Our anonymity is paramount to our cause. If people found out how many times our planet has been

visited by aliens, they'd lose it. It's our job to shield the world from that."

"That's all well and good, but how do you expect to help? You saw what it did to that city

in Nevada. It ripped through buildings and cars like they were made of paper," he said.

"We've accumulated some alien tech over the years." HR sounded like she was bragging.

"Our rule is to use what we need and store the rest."

"You have something to help me bring this nut down?"

"I think we have many things that would be beneficial to you."

"And you're just going to give them to me?"

"No. Borrow."

"If you do this all the time, why not stop him yourself?" Blair asked.

"Zealot is something new." HR moved around her desk to a cabinet on the far wall. "Every alien we've encountered has come and gone quietly. They come here for scientific research. Occasionally, they trade some of their tech for something we have and they want. None have

ever attacked us before." She entered a series of numbers on a keypad attached to the cabinet.

"But he's just one guy. Not an alien strike force," Eddie said.

"Before he gave his demands, we thought he might be the vanguard of an alien attack.

Testing our defenses." The lights on the keypad changed from white to green.

"And now you know he's here for me."

"Yes. And like I said, we can help." A hissing sound came from the wall behind the cabinet. It swung out of the way and revealed another hall. This one was well lit and led to a large

reinforced door.

"All right, let's see what you've got." Eddie couldn't contain his curiosity. If they had something that tipped the odds in his favor, then he'd take it. He and Blair followed HR down

the hall. The door opened automatically as she got near.

The room was large, about the size of an airplane hangar. There were crates of all sizes and materials. Small wooden ones with an American flag stamped on them, dated from the 1920's, were lined up along the edges of the room. Toward the center there were giant metal containers. Eddie reached his hand out and touched one. It didn't feel like he thought it would. It had some give to it, almost like rubber, but still had the cold metallic feel of steel. The walk around the

warehouse took several minutes. HR finally stopped next to a wooden crate.

"Is that some kind of alien language or bureaucrat shorthand?" Eddie asked.

She turned and laughed. "It's alien. You don't need to know anything other than that."

The crate stood about eight feet tall. Eddie wondered if there was an alien stored in it. HR waved her hand over a piece of metal on the box, and it lit up with a beeping sound. The lid opened and what was inside made their jaws drop. Blair reached out to touch it but pulled her hand back. Eddie moved closer. He wanted to make sure he was seeing what he thought he was

seeing.

"This is an alien exo-suit."

Blair giggled, she covered her mouth immediately and looked down in embarrassment. *She*

must be so giddy.

"This suit can enhance the user's strength and speed."

"It looks like something out of a science fiction movie," Eddie said. It was kind of silver

with blue boots and gloves. He leaned forward to see the back.

"It doesn't have a cape if that's what you're worried about," HR said.

"That's exactly what I was worried about," Eddie said.

HR and Blair both laughed. It was a good laugh. The tension had been heavy ever since

they got into the SUV back at Eddie's house, and it felt like it finally broke.

Blair wiped tears from her eyes. "I haven't laughed that hard in a long time."

"Why don't you have one of your guys wear this and go after Zealot?"

"Unfortunately, it doesn't react to human biology well."

"What do you mean by 'doesn't react well'?" Blair asked.

"It tends to burn out a normal human. They can last a few minutes in it, then their heart gives out. Too much stress on the body." HR waved her hand at the crate, and it closed with a
loud locking sound.

"I don't want to know how you figured that out," Eddie said.

"Short answer, voluntary experimentation." HR waved at them to follow her. They made their way back through the maze of crates to her office. "Tomorrow you'll try on the suit, and we'll see if you can last more than five minutes. My guess is you'll be able to wear this without
adverse effects." "Great. No pressure."

"Tomorrow?" Blair said.

"You'll be our guests until this situation is settled."

"Do we have a choice?" Eddie asked.

"No." HR sat down and started working on her computer.

CHAPTER THIRTEEN

B lair sat on the edge of the bed. The room they escorted her to wasn't bad. The bed was soft enough, and there was a large dresser, although she didn't bring anything to put in it. The bathroom was across from her. The lighting was old and dim, like it had been in the hallways. She laid down

and thought about the choices she made in her life that led her to this point.

In high school she was an introvert—did everything she could to stay under the radar. Her grades weren't outstanding but not poor either. B's and C's with the occasional A in mathematics. School was something to be tolerated. Her school offered full day vo-tech classes. And there was a long list of courses from horticulture, art, construction to different machine operating options. But

what Blair wanted was near the top of the alphabetical list—baking.

Blair loved to bake. It was her way to express her creativity. She dedicated a whole school year to hone her skills. She hoped to start up her own bakery someday. While she did well in her class, things didn't go the way she wanted them to. After graduation she applied

for jobs at several bakeries in and around her area. No one hired her. Lots of reasons were given, but none of them
    seemed legitimate.

Blair ended up taking a career path all too common for young girls—waitressing. It was fine for a while but not what she wanted long term. After a few years she started to bounce around to any job she thought looked better than the one she was in. Blair couldn't find satisfaction in any of them.

Desperate, she turned to a temp agency to find something that would give her a sense of purpose. She wanted a job she could feel good about at the end of the day. She embellished her qualifications
    on the paperwork and hoped they didn't look too close at her references either.

The agency told her they would call when a job opened up that matched her qualifications, but after three days, she still heard nothing. Maybe they found out she was a fraud. Maybe they called one of her references, and they told them the truth about her. Blair decided to call and make sure they hadn't forgotten about her. Just as she picked up her phone, it rang. She let out a scream and
    dropped the phone, then scrambled to pick it back up.

"Miss Benson?"

"Yes," she said. Her voice had a bit of desperation in it, so she took a deep breath and tried to
    play it cool.

"This is Tom from the temp agency."

"Oh, hello, Tom," she said in her cheeriest of voices.

"I'm calling to let you know we have a job placement for you."

"Great." *As long as it's not in a slaughterhouse, I'll take it*, she thought.

"It's a secretary position for a law firm. Does this sound like something you'd be interested in?"

"Yes. Very much so."

"Good. We're going to email you all the information. The time for your interview and

directions will also be attached."

"Thank you, Tom."

"You're welcome, Miss Benson. All we ask is that after your interview, please call and let us know how it went."

"Okay, I can do that." Blair danced around her living room with joy.

"Thank you again, Miss Benson, and good luck."

Blair put the phone down and flopped onto her couch. *Secretary, huh?* A fresh start. Life hadn't

been easy for her, and things were finally coming together.

Blair sat up on the bed and shook her head. All those decisions she made or didn't make. "And the rest, they say, is history," she said to no one.

With everything that happened in the last day, the fight she and Lester had felt like a lifetime ago. A mixture of guilt and sadness overwhelmed her. She hated the fact that she couldn't call him. She wanted to tell him why she said what she said. She wanted him to understand her thoughts. There was a nightstand with a drawer next to her bed. She pulled open the drawer. In it was a small bible, a channel listing for a TV that wasn't there, and a notepad with a pen. If she couldn't call him, she'd at least write down what she wanted him to know. She leaned back and wrote a letter that he

might never read.

* * *

Eddie walked into his room, and the door closed and locked behind him. HR's voice came out of a speaker in the far corner of the room. It sounded like she was talking to someone else at first,

then she directed the conversation to him.

"Mr. Solomon, I know you could bust through these doors, but I'm asking you for a little

cooperation and trust."

"Says the woman locking me in my room. Can you see me?" he asked. He waved his arms like

he was flagging down a rescue plane.

"No, but I can hear you. Rest up. Tomorrow we'll get you suited up and then go after Zealot.

The sooner we put this threat down, the better."

"All right. Thanks for the bedtime pep talk. See ya in the morning." A light on the speaker went

out. He guessed that meant the conversation was over.

Sweatpants and a t-shirt were set out on the edge of the bed. He put them on and laid down. He still tried to wrap his mind around everything that had happened to him. In the last few days, he

went from mild mannered P.I. to the only guy who can stop a superpowered psycho.

Between his bouts of anxiety and the pressure of Zealot—and now his brother—sleep was almost nonexistent for Eddie lately. But it came tonight. He dreamed of spaceships and alien planets—more of what he saw when he was struck by the beam. The vastness of the war was hard to comprehend. He stood on a strange planet and looked out at the night sky. His view of the moon and other planets was obscured by the wreckage of countless spaceships destroyed in the long

running war. From behind him, he heard a siren. It got louder and louder.

Eddie jerked up out of bed. The lights turned on and were excruciatingly bright. The alarm clock on the nightstand blared in his ear. He went to tap the snooze button, but instead he

inadvertently smashed the clock and turned the table to splinters.

"Wakey, wakey. It's day breaky." HR's chipper voice rang out of the speaker on the wall.

"I just went to sleep." Eddie rolled over and pulled the pillow over his head to block the light.

"You've been asleep for ten hours. Time to get up." A tone of urgency quickly replaced her

chipper voice. "Get dressed. Breakfast is waiting."

The clothes he wore the day before were gone. A set of blue overalls were in their place. *How'd they do that?* He grabbed them and made his way into the small bathroom to empty his bladder and

change. Even though HR said she couldn't see him, he wasn't taking any chances.

Eddie walked out of his room and found Agent Smith waiting for him. He was led to the cafeteria and saw Blair at table by herself. She looked up from her bowl of cereal and beckoned him over. He thought back to high school when his friends waved for him to join them.

"Good morning, sunshine," she said.

"Not you too." He sat down across from her and buried his face in his hands. Another agent came over to the table and asked if Eddie wanted anything for breakfast. "Coffee. Eggs. Toast.

Thank you." He waved at him dismissively and put his face back in his hands.

"Not enough sleep?" Blair asked.

"No, I had a weird dream." He looked at Blair with tired, bloodshot eyes." I was on a planet watching the aliens fight. Huge chunks of debris filled the sky. So much it was all I could see. It felt like I was there. I woke up exhausted." Blair reached across the table and took both of his hands.

His face softened, and he gave her a half smile. His food arrived and he started to eat.

"I wrote Lester a letter," she said with a smile. "It felt good to write down all the things I've

wanted to tell him. Very therapeutic. After that, I slept like a baby."

Eddie wondered if her optimism had a limit. This was a fight that he never wanted, but he was locked in. Blair could have bowed out at any time, and he would have understood completely. Yet here she was, going through this insanity with him, and she still managed to smile. Her positive

attitude seemed to be infecting him, and his outlook on the day brightened a little.

From out of the corner of his eye, he spotted movement. Things were about to get interesting.

"Good. You're going to need your energy." HR walked up to the table with two agents flanking

her. "After you're done eating, you'll be put in the suit. Let's see what happens, shall we?"

Blair jumped up. "Oh, I'm coming too! I wouldn't miss this for anything in the world."

Eddie chuckled. "Honestly, I can't wait to do this." He chased his toast with a swig of coffee

and stood up in front of HR.

"Really?" HR said.

"The sooner we can stop this alien nut job, the sooner I can go back to my life and some sense of normality." He hadn't even thought about the future, after this ended. Would he have a normal life? Would he keep the powers, or would they fade away? A flood of new thoughts and questions

filled his mind. He shook his head and forced himself to focus on the task at hand.

The walk to the warehouse seemed quicker than it was yesterday. The suit was out of the crate

already. The back of it was split open.

"All you have to do is walk in, and the suit will do the rest," HR said.

"What exactly is 'the rest'?" he asked.

"After you get in, it will close and adjust to your size. It never mattered who wore it. It would

shrink or grow to accommodate the wearer."

"That's so cool," Blair said, practically drooling.

Eddie turned and gave her a look of admonishment.

"What? It is." She grinned at him and went back to ogling at the suit.

"Whenever you're ready, Mr. Solomon." HR stepped out of the way and tapped on her computer pad. On the screen was an outline of the suit with strange symbols around it. There were bars off to the side with more of symbols under them. Eddie thought they might be used to gauge

his vitals and progress.

He took a deep breath and walked into the suit. The suit closed behind him with an odd metallic click. He wasn't ready for the way he felt in the suit. As it closed around him and sealed, he heard a hissing sound. The suit felt softer than he thought it would, bordering on comfy. Just based on first impressions, it he figured it would be hard and cold. The visor in his helmet lit up with the same strange alien writing on the crate. It blinked out for a second and returned, replacing the alien

words with English. He moved his arms around and marched in place. He jumped up and down a

little and bent over to touch his toes.

"What are you doing?" Blair asked.

"I'm warming up. You can't expect me to put on an alien super suit and not warm up a bit." He

gave HR a wink and went back to his stretches.

"It's an exo-suit, not a super suit," HR said, never taking her eyes off the pad.

"So, what do you need me to do first?"

A section of the roof opened up. She pointed in its direction. "I want you to fly up through that

opening and go as high as you can as fast as you can."

Eddie gave her a nod and took off.

CHAPTER FOURTEEN

A young woman stood outside the destroyed section of Reynolds, Nevada and reported on the aftermath of Zealot's attack. She spoke on the death toll and devastation he caused. Zealot watched the television with amusement.

"Eyewitnesses stated that the creature calling himself 'Zealot' came out of nowhere. One survivor close to the epicenter said he smiled just before the attack." Zealot filled with a sadistic sense of pride. The scene cut to video of him blowing up the police helicopter.

"News Copter 4 was able to get this video of Zealot shooting what appears to be red lightning at a police helicopter. He then turned to our cameraman and demanded a meeting with someone he called a 'champion.'"

"And I'm still waiting," Zealot said.

"No word on who this person is or what connection he or she has to this attack—"

Zealot turned the channel. Maybe another news program would have the Eoch's champion on. But it was the same clip of him talking to the camera again and another reporter giving the same information the last one did. He switched channels over and over, hoping to see his target. He

watched for hours with no revelation as to his target's identity. Then he blew up the television.

"Really? That's how you're going to handle this?" Bruce said.

"I did what you suggested. I found a populated area, destroyed it, and called him out when the

cameras showed up."

"It's a waiting game now. They know about you; they're probably trying to figure out what you are and how to take you down."

"I want the champion!" Zealot exclaimed. The gem in his chest glowed brighter. Sparks of red energy shot off him and burnt small holes in what was left of the farmhouse that he'd been hiding

out in.

"Calm down. They could have planes out looking for you. If one flies over and sees red

lightning bolts shoot out of the roof, you'll be had."

"I don't care about that. I need to find the other." Zealot swung his hand at his ghostly adviser. He began to pace around the living room. Somewhere in his mind the Thiar put a desire in him to find and kill the other champion. The longer he went without completing his task, the more it

wound him up. It took everything Zealot had to keep his composure.

"Lucky for you I have a plan B," Bruce said.

"Why should I listen to you again?" he asked.

"Because you still don't know who you're looking for, and I have an idea that will get him to

drop everything and come running."

"And what is that?"

"One word. Hostages." Bruce gave a grin that reminded Zealot of someone he used to know

but couldn't quite remember.

Zealot wondered what kind of a person his opposite was. He hoped he or she would be the kind that showed up to help innocent people. And when they did, he'd be ready to use that

weakness against them. "You have any thoughts on where I should do this?"

"I do," Bruce said. Then silence.

Zealot rolled his eyes and waited. His jaw clenched as time stood still. "Well, are you going to

share anytime soon?"

"Not sure why, but I remember a spot I used—I mean, we used to go to in our former life. I'll show you the way."

Zealot catapulted himself into the air and flew to Bruce's mystery spot.

* * *

Dark clouds moved in. It was going to be a raw and rainy Saturday. This wouldn't stop the crowds of people who waited all week for the stands at the farmers' market to open. Fresh fruits and vegetables, homemade crafts and baked goods as far as the eye could see. A light rain

started to fall.

Arthur Madison was a regular at the market. Since he retired a few years back, he turned into a faithful shopper. As he walked through the aisles, the vendors and other shoppers waved

and chatted him up a little.

"Looks like we might get a storm today," one of the vendors called out.

"I don't think so." Arthur waved a dismissive hand at him and laughed. "I heard it was

going to miss us. We'll get some rain but not the heavy stuff."

A rumble of thunder made its way through the crowd. Arthur looked up and a streak of lightning moved across the sky. He took his glasses off and rubbed his eyes. "I must be tired or seeing things," he said to no one in particular. Another lightning bolt lit the sky, but it was red

this time. Little did he know today would be his last trip to the market.

* * *

Zealot's enhanced vision allowed him to see the large gathering of people from his vantage point. He plotted where he wanted to strike. He almost pitied the people below. Almost. He was a god to them, he could spare their lives or take them at his leisure. *After I kill the other champion, I will be their god.* A benevolent ruler, as long as they followed his every command.

Disobedience would have grave consequences.

He dropped out of the sky and into the crowd. His landing caused the ground to quake. People and stands fell. Everyone ran for their lives. This was the monster they had seen on TV,

after all.

"Stop," Zealot screamed. All the glass in the area shattered. People fell clutching their ears.

"If you value your pathetic lives, you will remain still, or I will relieve you of them."

An old man got up and started to run. Zealot pointed a finger at him. His hand glowed red,

then a bolt of lightning tore through his target. The body spun in the air and landed with a thud.

People screamed and cried until he shouted again. "Silence," he said. Red sparks flew off of

him in every direction. An eerie silence fell over the market.

He walked among the crowd, pleased with himself. He made his way to a couple holding each other. The fear in their eyes was palpable, and it sent a pleasing shudder down his back. He leaned down, took the woman by the throat, and lifted her to her feet. Her husband got up and

faced Zealot.

"Ready to die for her? Hmm? You will bring me a reporter, or she dies. How's that? I will

be heard." Zealot pushed the man. "Off you go. Hurry back now."

Zealot heard sirens in the distance. If they didn't interfere with his business, he'd allow them to live. A hostage situation of this magnitude, once televised, would certainly bring the

champion to him.

Waiting made him restless. It hadn't been that long since he sent the man out, but he should've been back by now. Zealot's hand pulsed with a red glow when he heard the crowd's rumblings shift. The husband, sweaty and out of breath, worked his way back through the sea of people—a reporter and cameraman right behind him. Zealot threw the woman at her husband's feet. The man helped her up, and they moved away in a hurry as the reporter stepped forward. She signaled her cameraman to start filming and aimed her microphone toward Zealot. "Who are you? What do you want?" she asked, wide-eyed. Her voice cracked a bit.

"You may call me Zealot. As for what I want, that takes a bit of explaining."

CHAPTER FIFTEEN

E ddie flew farther and faster than he ever did before. He wasn't sure how far HR expected him to go, but with the exo-suit, going to the moon seemed like a viable option. Everything felt effortless.

He looked down and saw the curvature of the Earth. A readout in the visor of his helmet read

53,000 feet and just over 600 mph.

"How's it going?" HR said through his earpiece.

Eddie was at a loss for words. This was an experience like no other—something he never thought possible. There was no way for him to convey that to HR or anyone. For one moment, Eddie thought hard about not stopping, seeing just how far he could go. There was nothing holding him there. Lester and Blair would miss him, sure, but that was it. No strings, no commitments. Just

keep going and see what's out there.

"Fine." He turned his focus back on learning what the suit could do. The readout on his visor

told him he was at just under 74,000 feet. "How far did you want me to go?"

"According to my data, you're about fourteen miles up. How do you feel?"

"Great. It's an awesome view from here." He wished he could capture the moment and share it
with Blair and the others.

"I'm sure it is. We'll need to..." There was a click, then silence.

Eddie tapped the side of the helmet. "Hello? Is everything okay?"

After a minute or so, HR came back online. "You need to get back here. Zealot showed up.

He's in Kansas City. He's taken hostages and gave you an hour to show up or he'll start killing them.

Get down here now."

Eddie turned and headed back toward Earth. "I'm still not sure what other capabilities this suit has. What else should I know about it?"

"There's not much else to figure out, Mr. Solomon. Like I said before, it augments the user's
abilities. That's all." The connection went dead.

Eddie cursed under his breath. He pushed himself harder and exploded forward even faster. Taking hostages was a strategy used by cowards or the very desperate. And Zealot seemed the desperate type. He had to stop this maniac, and soon. He knew he needed to be smart about it. Going in guns blazing wasn't the right way. If he failed, Zealot was sure to use his powers on the
world. And the world wasn't ready to deal with someone—or something—like that.

Just before Eddie broke through the clouds, a shock coursed through his suit. The view on his visor went dark, then came back up. Now was not the time for this thing to act up. He could see the
forest he flew out of but no building. A blue line showed up in his vision.

"Follow the line." It was HR. "It'll show you the way here."

He adjusted his trajectory to fall in line with the guide. Minutes later he flew through the opening of the warehouse and touched down several feet from the group. Another shock hit, and

before he could say anything, a burning pain ripped through his chest.

* * *

"Amazing! What a success!" Blair cheered and clapped for Eddie landing. But her celebration was short lived as she watched him fall to one knee. She turned to HR. "Will he be okay?"

HR and a few agents ran to him. Two of them grabbed him under his arms. HR tapped her pad. The suit opened up, and Eddie spilled out. The front of his shirt was burnt away. His chest looked like he had been hit with an explosive—a black center and gray scarring moved out from it. His eyes

rolled up into his head as he fell to the ground. He didn't even try to catch himself.

"What's wrong?" Blair said. She ran to him, but Jones stopped and restrained her. She kicked

and twisted, trying to free herself. "Let me go. I need to help him."

"There's nothing you can do," the agent said.

HR bent down over him and placed two fingers to his wrist. "Get the doctor. Put him in the

emergency transport with the medical team."

"Where are you taking him? "Blair asked.

"We have less than an hour to get to Kansas City and keep Zealot from killing possibly

hundreds of hostages."

"You're taking him to Zealot?" She couldn't believe what she heard.

"We don't have any other options right now." HR turned to a group of agents. "Load up the

suit. It's coming too."

"Ma'am, is that wise?" Smith asked. "He lasted longer than any other subject, but it still fried
him."

"Unlike the others, he's still breathing. There's a chance he'll pull through. If he doesn't, we'll
need every advantage we can get—even if I have to wear that infernal thing myself."

Eddie moaned. He lay on a stretcher being pushed to the ambulance. HR put her ear close to
hear him. He made some mumbling noises, but she shook her head.

"What did you say? Mr. Solomon? Tell me." She leaned in.

In a barely audible tone, he said, "L-L-Lester. Get... Lester."

"Get him on that truck now! Smith, you're with me. Let's go!" HR said.

"Wait!" Blair yelled. "I'm going too!" But no one answered her.

The medical team hurried to load Eddie onto the transport. The truck roared to life and sped
away. As they drove off, it looked like they disappeared through a bright light.

Blair turned and grabbed Jones. "I need to be there. He needs his friends."

Jones looked around. She could tell he was contemplating something. The other agents readied for battle, packing up weapons and putting on special gear. He pulled Blair out of the way of the commotion.

"Come on," he said. They made their way through the maze of crates and shelving to a garage.

"This is a bad idea, but you're right. He'll need someone he trusts."

"No... You want to use me to get him to fight Zealot. Even after that suit almost killed him." She pulled away from his grip. She wasn't about to help send her friend into a fight he might not
survive.

"Do you want to go or not?" Jones stood stone still.

She hated being used like that, but it was the only way to get to Eddie. "Fine. Let's go." They

hopped into the car. "Wait. How far is Kansas City? We'll never make it in time."

"Don't worry. I have that covered." He turned the key, and the engine roared. Lights around what looked like a garage door came to life and started to pulsate. A golden shimmer covered the opening. Jones typed something in on his tablet, and the shimmer pulsated with the lights. He

looked at Blair. "This will feel kind of weird."

"What will?"

Jones hit the accelerator, and they passed through the shimmer. It was as if a glitter bomb just went off. An explosion of color whirled around the car. She only saw a fragmented rainbow in a sea

of blackness, and then it stopped. To her right, a large arching sign read, 'Farmers' Market.'

"What? How?" Before Jones replied, she opened the door and threw up her breakfast.

"I warned you it would feel weird. Thank you for not getting sick in the car." She couldn't tell if

that was sarcasm or him trying to be funny. "We need to wait here."

"But what about Eddie? You said—"

"I said we'd need your help. But not yet." Jones gave her a stern look.

Blair sat back in her seat and looked down at her lap. She felt like she was seven again

and her father just scolded her for not listening.

* * *

The medical transport was more akin to a box truck than an ambulance. Traditional methods for taking care of injuries wouldn't work on Eddie's particular physiology. The transport carried alien equipment able to help him. He was contained in what looked like a glass

coffin. Various screens and keypads were attached around it.

HR sat in the corner of the transport, trying to stay out of the way, but kept a close eye on Eddie. The doctor stood at the foot of his case and tapped some buttons on the screen. Red, blue, and green lasers crisscrossed his body. A nurse came along side and injected a clear liquid into the case, and it dispersed into gas once inside. Eddie tensed up and seized. His arms and legs stiffened. He arched his back, then relaxed. The sound of his heart emitted through a set of

speakers at the head of the capsule.

"How is he?" HR asked.

"I'm surprised he's still alive. How long was he in the suit?"

"Almost an hour. What's his prognosis? When can we put him back in the suit?"

"He's strong, but the suit won't be an option for him." The doctor moved around Eddie

and examined the different readouts that popped up on the glass case.

"Are you sure?"

The doctor turned to HR. "The other subjects all lasted a few minutes in that thing. You

know how they turned out."

"Black as a cinder. Their bodies turned to charcoal."

"And all Eddie got was a burn mark like a starburst. His biology is still mostly a mystery to

me. The fact that we've been able to stabilize and treat him is a small miracle."

"Stabilizing isn't enough. He needs to stop Zealot. Now." HR took a step toward the doctor. "How soon can he go?"

"Go? I told you he's lucky to be breathing, let alone able to fight a monster." He shook his head and continued to check Eddie's vital signs.

"I don't care how you do it. Have him ready in ten minutes." Before the doctor could object, HR held her hand out. Her patience had worn thin. She pulled her phone out and hit the

call button.

A voice answered. "Yes?"

"Agent Smith, take your men and keep Zealot occupied. I'm sending in another group to

secure the hostages. Do you understand?"

"Yes. Smith out."

HR put her phone in her pocket. She walked to the rear of the transport and opened the

door. She turned back to the doctor. "Ten minutes. I'll send some agents for him."

The doctor shrugged his shoulders and nodded. He and his nurse got back to work.

* * *

Smith and the other agents were a quarter mile away from Zealot and the hostages. Smith worked in the Cloak division, but was leading a Dagger unit to engage Zealot. Normally, Cloak agents dealt with investigation and Dagger units were more militaristic. They usually operated separately, but this was an extraordinary circumstance. All hands were on deck. Smith and his unit moved quickly and took positions outside the market. They were equipped with blaster

rifles powerful enough to take down large alien threats. Zealot was something else though.

HR watched her men on her tablet. She stood by the transport and looked toward the market. A dark figure hovered over the frightened crowd. Smith and the Dagger unit were red dots on the screen. With a tap, they turned green. She watched a dozen lasers strike Zealot from all sides. The area lit up like a small sun. Zealot flew up out of the laser fire and launched red lightning at her men. Twelve green dots became ten, then six. She pressed a call button on her pad.

"Fall back," she shouted. "Find a new vantage point and continue firing."

Another Dagger unit showed up to reinforce the remaining six. HR gave the command and more laser fire hit the target. They kept a constant stream on him. She couldn't see anything but a ball of white light, until Zealot fought back.

CHAPTER SIXTEEN

Z ealot hovered over the market and scanned the horizon. If his opponent had any empathy for the hostages, they'd be here at any moment. The dozen figures moving around just outside the market didn't go unnoticed. He figured an attack from them was inevitable. But nothing was going to alter his plans. The champion would show up, a fight would ensue, and Zealot would reign supreme.

Suddenly, a hot white light surrounded him. *Lasers*, he thought to himself. While the heat was uncomfortable, it didn't cause any real pain. Whatever the Thiar did to him numbed his body to pain. Not able to see what really annoyed him, Zealot flew up out of the path of the beams. *Just as I thought.* Twelve soldiers took aim, laser dots riddled his chest. He held his arms out and sent red lightning to strike down his uninvited guests. Small explosions blasted off where the lightning hit. The soldiers burst into flames. Any remaining forces retrained their beams on him, but their effort was futile.

More soldiers arrived, this time with rocket launchers. One hit Zealot in the back. He spun end over end without any damage to his body. "That was fun, but I need more. Bring me the champion."

He locked on to one of the men holding a laser weapon and flew straight at him. He grabbed him by his arm and dragged him along the ground. Zealot's sharp fingernails sunk in like a shark bite. He flew past a few other soldiers, turned around, and threw their comrade at them. The group went

down like bowling pins.

He flew back over and another group opened fire on him. He stretched open his mouth and shrieked. The force of the attack shredded four or five men, and the others in the area fell to their knees, hands pressed to ears.

He liked this. It was a nice warm up to get him ready for the other. Zealot flew over the market

again and hovered there.

"I don't know who you are," he screamed, "but thank you for the work out." He looked down and noticed the hostages were gone. They weren't there to kill him, only distract him. "What did you

do with my hostages?"

He pulled himself into a ball and lightning formed a shell around him. A few seconds later, he threw open his arms and lightning flew in every direction. Large sections of the farmers' market disintegrated and the rest caught fire. Cars in the parking lot blew away like autumn leaves. Windows

blew out from surrounding buildings.

"The champion will show himself, or I will destroy this entire city," he said.

Zealot watched as people ran through the smoke and rubble. They looked like rats abandoning

a sinking ship. All but one. That one walked toward him.

"This is it." he said. A demonic smile grew on his face, and he propelled himself at his enemy.

 * * *

The door of the transport swung open, and HR burst through. The medical team still swarmed Eddie, but now he was sitting on the examination table. She walked toward the table, and the doctor stopped her.

"He's not fully healed yet."

"That's not my problem." HR pushed her way past the doctor and put her hands on Eddie's

shoulders. "Our people are getting slaughtered, and he's our only hope."

"If you send him out now, he could die. Then we'll have no hope."

HR ignored the doctor and his advice. "Mr. Solomon, you need to get out there. Now." She

showed him video of the last few minutes. "We're getting beat bad. We need you."

Eddie let himself down off the table, took a deep breath, and stretched. "I heard."

"Then you know what you have to do." She grabbed a pair of sweatpants and t-shirt and tossed

them to him. "Get dressed, and stop that maniac."

While Eddie was getting ready, the doors opened again. This time it was Blair. She ran over and

wrapped her arms around him.

"Ouch. Easy. I'm still a little sore." He gave her a smile and a wink.

"You're not thinking of going out there, are you?" Blair asked.

"I'm fine. I've got to stop Zealot."

"Are you, though? Look at that scar on your chest. Can't you try another day?"

"Crazy people rarely keep schedules. Superpowered ones even less. I need to take him down

now."

"Where's Agent Jones? Wasn't he with you?" HR asked.

"He was right behind me."

Explosions rocked the transport, shaking it side to side. HR hit the call button on her pad.

"What's going on out there?"

An anxious voice answered her. "I'm running interference until Mr. Solomon is ready." It was

Jones.

"How are you going to slow him down when the others couldn't?" But she already knew.

"Don't do this, Agent Jones. He is ready to go. There's no reason to put yourself in harm's way."

"Putting myself in harm's way is what my life is all about." With that, the connection went dead.

HR jumped out of the transport and found the exo-suit missing. She looked to the sky and

watched Jones and Zealot clash in midair.

* * *

Eddie jumped out of the transport and headed for Zealot. Even though he answered the doctor's questions and was cleared, he still felt sore. This was a new kind of pain for him—one,

he hoped, he'd never have to feel again.

Jones and Zealot tumbled through the air. They pushed off each other and both spun out of control. Eddie jumped into the air and rocketed toward them, hoping to catch Zealot off

guard.

Zealot got himself under control just as Eddie flew by and landed a punch square into his chest. He started the somersaults again. Eddie went in for another go, but Jones flew past and

continued the fight.

"You don't need do this, Jones," Eddie yelled.

But Jones either didn't hear him or wouldn't listen. He flew right into Zealot and was

swatted away like a bug.

The villain turned and flew straight for Eddie. "I knew you'd show, champion. I didn't

expect you to bring help."

"Not my call, gruesome." Eddie's body ached. His chest felt like it was on fire, again. But

he knew if Zealot got away or worse, won, things would get much worse for everyone on Earth.

They charged each other again, but this time Zealot got the upper hand. He charged up his

fist with his lightning and knocked Eddie almost a half mile away.

* * *

Jones recovered from his hit and took to the air. *Oh, no you don't,* Zealot thought. He threw red lightning at Jones, sending him into a line of parked cars. The impact knocked the man out. Zealot was on top of him in a matter of seconds. He grabbed the faceplate of the helmet and tore it off. His eyes sparked with red energy. Jones groaned.

"This is for helping the champion try to cheat me out of my win," Zealot said, his voice

like fingernails on a chalkboard.

Jones winced. "You're the one who's going to lose." Blood dripped from his mouth, and

he spit at Zealot.

Anger gripped Zealot in a way it never had before. He thrust his claw-like fingers through the suit and into Jones' chest, then lifted him up over his head. "I never lose." Zealot threw him

to the ground in disgust and drove his heel into his face, caving in his head.

The suit began to glow, and before Zealot knew what was happening, it exploded. He was thrown with a force he didn't expect, and it hurt—the first real pain he felt since his conversion. He looked down and saw blood—his blood. Shards of the suit were embedded into his chest, arms, and legs. The amount of blood he was losing troubled him. He needed to regroup. He took in the destruction and carnage around him. Even though he didn't kill the champion, now he knew his identity. He'd find him later and finish the job.

* * *

Eddie made his way back just in time to see Zealot fly off. He wanted to chase him down, but the pain in his chest was almost unbearable. Eddie was a bloody mess. For only fighting Zealot for a short time, he took a lot of damage. His knuckles bled. The side of his face was swollen and bruised.

Blair and HR came out of the transport.

"He's gone," Eddie said. With that, all the strength left his body, and he collapsed. Three agents came from around the truck and helped him up.

"We'll get him. We just need some more time," HR said.

"We'll get him?" Eddie used what little strength he had left and punched the side of the transport, causing it to slide several hundred feet from where it was. "We're not doing anything. You've done quite enough as it is."

"Without us, Zealot would have killed the hostages and god knows who else." HR pushed her chest out, trying to assume a position of authority, but Eddie wasn't buying it.

He walked over and leaned down to her level. "Let's get one thing straight. All this damage is on you. The scar on my chest and almost dying is on you. For an organization that's supposedly secret, well, you certainly blew that, and that's on you too."

HR began to argue, but he shot up into the sky.

* *

HR tapped her pad furiously, then stopped. The tracking device she planted on him indicated that he was in the transport. Eddie must have found the chip at some point and

tossed it. She didn't worry. She found him once, she can do it again.

"Send agents to his home and all known locations he might go," HR said. She waved her

hand, and the remaining agents scattered.

"I don't think he wants your help," Blair said.

"I don't care what he wants." She pushed her finger into Blair's chest. "The safety of this planet is at risk, and he's our best and only hope of protecting it. So, if you'll excuse us, Miss Benson." She pushed her way past Blair and back into the transport. The engine roared to life

and was on its way.

* * *

"Hey, what about me?" Blair ran after the transport and waved her arms, but it was no use.

Local law enforcement, first responders, and news crews came her way. She walked through what was left of the farmers' market and searched for survivors. But the agents Zealot

killed, including Agent Jones, were gone. She didn't even see them collect the bodies.

No time in her life had she ever felt so helpless and alone. Abandoned in a strange place with death and destruction all around her, Blair crumpled to the ground and sobbed

uncontrollably.

CHAPTER SEVENTEEN

I t still hurt every time he visited, but it was the only place where Eddie found peace. He knelt by his wife's tombstone and felt shame for leaving her by herself for so long. It was a silly thought.

She was dead, yet the thought haunted him.

"Just one more bad decision in a long line of bad decisions." Eddie turned and sat down on the damp, dew covered grass. He leaned against Emma's stone. "I'm sorry. I know I've probably said that a lot since you died."

He was glad for the lack of traffic or people. It was three in the morning, and the cemetery was outside the city. A strange kind of oasis away from the rest of the world. "Have I got a story for you." Eddie went on and told Emma all about moving to Philadelphia, being recruited by a race of aliens to be their champion, and the quagmire his life had become since then.

The pain in his chest wasn't any better. He lifted his shirt to look at the scar again. He touched it, but the pain didn't come from his injury. His anxiety was to blame. "With all the upgrades the Eoch gave me, you'd think this would've been taken care of. But here we are." Eddie closed his eyes and took deep breaths. *In through the nose. Hold it. Out through the mouth.* He imagined himself with Emma and their son, or daughter. The picture changed depending on his mood. This was his happy

place. Somewhere he could fight off the anxiety and depression.

He and Emma sat on their back porch and watched their kid play. He ran out and chased them around, then fell and let them jump on him. In the years following the accident, his therapist suggested imagining his family, but it never really helped. If anything, it made things worse— picturing a life he could never have. *Not much of a happy place.* It was no wonder he gave up on it. He buried the past deep down and did his best to forget it. It always found a way back though. Sirens and flashing lights would set him off. He avoided the news because a similar story would cause the anxiety to hit. He did his best to isolate himself—left his home and moved across the country just so

he wouldn't see the constant reminders of his old life.

He immersed himself in mindless work to keep stray thoughts from sneaking up on him. Yet with all the things he did, all the medicine he was given, nothing kept the ghosts at bay. He was

haunted nightly with visions of fire and death, helpless to do anything about it.

The only way to free himself from it was to check out. Shuffle off this mortal coil. He had a plan, several plans actually—walking out in front of a bus, running his car into a tree and conveniently 'forgetting' to buckle his seat belt. As a law enforcement officer, he saw all kinds of suicides. He had quite a list of ideas on how to do it. The night he was hit with the beam was supposed to be the night—one last meal with his brother, then home to choose which way he'd off

himself.

Fate, if there was such a thing, had other plans and conspired to keep him alive. Now he found himself here, in the middle of a cemetery, licking his wounds. He wiped his tears and glanced up to find an old man staring at him from a few rows away. He had long, stringy white hair with a long beard to match. There were a lot of homeless people in and around LA. It was only natural for them to seek out a place like this—quiet and out of the way, no one to hassle them. But there was something off about this one. Before Eddie could put a finger on it, the man walked toward him. "You okay? I heard you crying. Thought I'd check on you."

Eddie wiped his eyes. "I'm fine," he said.

"If you want to talk about it..."

"Let me stop you there." Eddie didn't like being interrupted. He was there to think and try to come to an understanding of what just happened in Kansas City. And to his own life. "I'm here to be alone. So, if you'd please."

"I understand." The man pointed a bony finger at him." I know desperation when I see it."

"What makes you think I'm desperate?"

"Sitting in a cemetery. At night. Crying over a grave. You are a desperate man."

"What's your name?" Eddie was emotionally spent. He didn't want to argue with the stranger all night. He wanted to end this conversation quickly.

"Merle."

"Well, Merle, whether or not I'm desperate is none of your concern." He pulled his knees to his chest and buried his head in his hands.

"Do you push everyone away or just the tattered-looking ones?"

Eddie looked up at Merle. He clenched his jaw and scowled. His bright blue eyes glowed even brighter. "I've had a rough couple of years. And the last few weeks have been even more stressful."

Merle continued as if he didn't notice Eddie's obvious disgust. "I know you. I saw you on TV. You were fighting that monster in Kansas City. You guys did a number on that market."

Eddie never thought about being recorded. Something that big and destructive would definitely have eyes on it. Any thought of staying under the radar was most likely gone. This was a new problem he'd have to deal with.

"News or phone?"

"What?"

"Was the video of me from the news, or did someone use their phone?"

"Oh. Both. There were a few different angles of your fight. What was that thing?"

"Same as me. Kind of. It's a long story."

"I have time." Merle moved a little closer and sat down.

Eddie noticed Merle didn't have anything with him. Most of the homeless he encountered when he was with the LAPD had everything they owned with them—shopping cart, wagon, backpack.

Their possessions were sacred. Merle just had the clothes on his back. Clothes that were really dirty.

They looked like they used to be a white shirt and pants in a former life. And he was barefoot. If Merle was homeless, he was the oddest homeless man he'd ever met.

He told Merle the story of his life, about the aliens, and what he was supposed to do. Merle took it all in and nodded every now and then. It felt kind of good to talk about it. Without realizing it, the pain in his chest was gone.

"I'm no shrink, but I think I know what the problem is," Merle said.

"Please. Do tell." Sarcasm dripped from the words. Eddie couldn't wait to hear this.

"You're ungrateful."

The words shocked Eddie to his core. *Who is he to say that?* His life had been undone in ways this man couldn't possibly understand. "I'm sorry? What do you mean I'm ungrateful?"

"You had a good life that was unfortunately taken away from you. But instead of grieving and being grateful for what you still had, you went and wrapped yourself in self-pity." Merle leaned back against another headstone and folded his arms.

Eddie was furious. He sprang to his feet and leaned in toward Merle. "You watch your mouth.

You don't know what I've been through."

"Think about it," Merle said. "When was the last time you were thankful for something or grateful for someone?"

"My brother helped me when I moved back home. I'm grateful for him."

"Then why are you sitting here among the dead and not with him having this talk?"

Revelation hit Eddie like a sledgehammer to the head. He looked around like he had just woken up from a dream. While he at one point planned to end his life physically, he ended it emotionally the night Emma died. He was a walking corpse just going through the motions. Never thankful for what he still had. He buried his soul with his wife and their unborn child and walked away a living dead man. Merle saw it too. Eddie realized that he was just a shell of who he had been.

"Who are you?" Perhaps Merle was an angel, and Eddie was experiencing an 'It's a wonderful life' moment.

"Someone who has lived a long life. Long enough to see the despair in you and how to help turn you around." Merle got to his feet but not without some trouble. Eddie could tell he was in some pain. "Your life won't turn around overnight, but now you have a foundation on which to build a new one."

Eddie reached out and shook his hand. "Thank you." He didn't think those words were enough, but they were all he had. "Have you thought about making a career out of this?"

"Not again," Merle said.

"What?"

"Nevermind."

Eddie heard sirens in the distance. He didn't know if another anxiety attack was on its way, but he refused to let that stop him. Since he was in LA, he had an idea who the responders might be. He turned to thank Merle one more time, but the man was gone. Eddie thought he saw the fading of

twinkling white light where Merle had stood. He shook it off and jumped into the air.

It wasn't a complete fix, but it was a good place to start. As much as it hurt him to put the past behind him, it'd be worth it to finally have a future free from pain—it had to be. He understood there was a long road ahead to a full recovery. But he couldn't wait to get back to Philly to start his

new life.

Grateful. This was something his therapist never spoke of. All they did was focus on the past. How did it make him feel? How was he coping with it? Reminder after reminder of his loss. Now it was time to appreciate what he still had and build on a new future.

CHAPTER EIGHTEEN

B lair woke up in the triage area of the hospital. She found it difficult to keep her eyes open. *What happened after Eddie left?* She vaguely recalled HR and her agents leaving, but everything after that was hazy. Lights and sirens flashed in her mind. She rolled over to go back to sleep but jumped

up with a stabbing pain in her shoulder. She reached over and felt a small sore spot.

"Where am I?" Blair became fully awake. She knew she was in a hospital, but she didn't know where or why. *And where are my clothes?* She wore a hospital gown, and a number of cords were stuck to her arms and chest. She sat up and saw that she wasn't in a private room. There were curtains

dividing her from other patients.

She ripped the wires from her skin. They were also around her ankles and head. The machine

that monitored her blood pressure and pulse started to beep.

A nurse rushed in. "Ma'am, you need to lie back down." The nurse took the wires from Blair

and reattached them.

"I don't want to lie down. I need to go home."

"Ma'am, you were found in the wreckage of the farmers' market. The doctors want to make sure you aren't injured." The nurse tried to lay Blair back down, but she resisted. The nurse stepped

back. "Okay, easy".

"I was there after the damage was done."

"The first responders claimed they found you on the ground crying and calling out for someone. They gave you a sedative when you became violent and uncooperative." Blair didn't remember any

of that. Was she telling the truth?

"Where am I?"

"Grand Oak Medical Center."

"And when can I speak to a doctor?"

"I was hoping you'd talk to me first." A woman in a pants suit and jacket came in from around the curtain. She reached into her pocket and pulled out a badge and I.D. "I'm Detective Louise Hunt. Can you tell me what happened?" She pulled out a pen and a small notepad.

Blair didn't know where to begin. There was no way she'd talk about Eddie and his powers. And trying to explain the secret government agency that dealt with aliens was completely out of the

question, not to mention the teleporting garage door.

"I'm not sure what happened." Blair didn't like lying. Not that she was morally opposed to it,

she was just bad at it.

"Miss. Benson, we have witnesses that tell us you were found in the wreckage, but you had

no injuries."

"I know. I was one of the lucky ones." She rubbed her shoulder where she was given her

shot.

"Did you see the people responsible for causing the damage?"

Over the detective's shoulder, the current news report showed up on the television. Video of Zealot and an armored Jones fighting played on the screen. The video cut to Zealot swooping in and attacking the Cloak and Dagger agents, then Eddie flew in. The video paused

every now and then and zoomed in on their faces. Eddie's face was clearly visible.

"Do you know that man?" Detective Hunt asked.

"Who? Him? No," Blair said and turned from the screen.

"There's something you're not telling me. Right now, you're not in any trouble, but if you know something that can help with our investigation and you withhold it, I can have you

arrested."

Blair tired of the questions and wanted this to end. She remembered what Lester told her

about what the police could and couldn't do.

"I know my rights, Detective. I didn't do anything wrong. I was just in the wrong place at the wrong time and got caught up in the attack. Unless you're charging me with something, I'm

leaving."

Detective Hunt closed the notepad and walked toward the curtain. She stopped and turned

around. "You sure there's nothing you want to say?"

Blair shook her head and slid out of the bed to get her clothes. As the detective walked out,

Blair let out a sigh of relief and fell into the chair.

"You sounded great. Maybe you should be a lawyer."

Blair looked up and saw Lester standing there. She leapt out of the chair and ran over to him. With all that happened to her today, she was a roller coaster of emotions. While in Lester's

arms, she let go and cried.

"It's okay. I'm here."

"How did you know to come here?"

"I got a call from one of those agents. They told me Eddie was hurt and that he asked for me. When I got off the plane, an agent brought me here and told me where I could find you.

Where is Eddie?"

"It's a long story. He's fine. Kind of."

"Kind of? That doesn't really tell me anything."

"I'll tell you everything on the way home. You will take me home, won't you?" Blair stuck

her lip out and gave him a pouty look.

Lester laughed. "Of course. Blair, I never wanted things to spiral out of control like they did. I said some dumb things, but I want us to work this out. I love you." Blair threw her arms around him again. She squeezed him so tight that he had to pry her off him. "Don't break me.

Last thing I want is to have to be checked in here too."

"Sorry," she said." Give me a minute to get dress, and then we'll go. And Lester?"

"Yes?"

"I love you too."

* * *

Instead of flying back to Philadelphia, Lester opted to rent a car and drive. He thought they could use the time to relax and have a mini vacation. Blair filled him in on everything—every minor detail—from being picked up with Eddie to the secret base and up to the fight with Zealot. Lester took it all in. He decided not to chastise her about the bad decisions she made.

He was happy to get her back, and the last thing he wanted was another argument.

"So, Eddie flew off, and the Cloak and Dagger people left you there by yourself?"

"Yep. Until I heard your voice, I wasn't sure what I was going to do."

"Well, we have a drive ahead of us. I'll find a hotel. We can get a nice dinner, sleep, then

get back on the road and be home by tomorrow evening."

Blair leaned over and gave Lester a kiss. She reclined her seat and rolled over a bit. "I think

I'll get a head start on that sleep."

"Okay. I'll wake you when we get to the hotel."

Lester played it cool and seemed to be taking everything in stride, but inside he was furious. How could Eddie take his girlfriend into such a dangerous situation? If he wanted to go head long into a predicament that risked injury, he should've gone by himself. Dragging innocent people with him was fool-hardy and stupid. Lester wouldn't forget this.

He parked the car and gave Blair a gentle shake. Before she had a chance to acknowledge him, he was already making his way to the passenger side. Lester opened the door for her as she

put up her seat.

"We have arrived," he said. It wasn't the five-star hotel he'd hoped for, but he was feeling

drowsy. The small Holiday Inn would have to do for the night.

"I'm starving," Blair said. "I hope there's a restaurant close."

"There's a diner across the street. After we check in, we'll go over and eat."

"Perfect. Then we can go to our room and... relax." Blair took Lester's hand and she

pulled him into the hotel.

All throughout dinner, she flirted with him—a sly smile or subtle caress. Lester didn't know

what'd gotten into her. She wasn't usually as forward as she'd been tonight.

"Lester, are you blushing?" she asked and giggled.

"No." He put his finger in his shirt collar and loosened it. "It's kind of warm in here, and

the food is hot." He gave her a smile back.

"I thought I might've been embarrassing you."

"Come on. I can stand in a courtroom all day with the worst of humanity, who have done god knows what, and it doesn't faze me." He sat up a little straighter, hoping to project an air of

importance."

"Oh, well," she said, "I'll have to try harder."

Lester's eyes widened, and he took a large gulp of water. He wasn't sure how to take her

new attitude.

They headed back to their room after dinner. Blair grabbed his wrist, turning him around,

and kissed him—a deep, passionate kiss that he was not ready for.

"Blair, I—"

"Don't say anything." She led him to the bedroom.

They made love like teenagers that night. The experience overwhelmed them both, and

they fell into a deep sleep.

* * *

Blair woke up and rolled over to cuddle with Lester like she always did after a night of lovemaking. She reached out and found the bed empty. There was a note on the bedside table:

Blair. Went out to grab breakfast. Be back soon. Love, Lester.

She put the note down and took a shower. By the time she was done, Lester was back. There were bagels and coffee on the table. She stepped out of the bathroom in one of the robes the hotel provided. She ran to Lester and jumped on him, knocking him backward onto the bed.

She kissed him, but he rolled her off.

"What's wrong?" she asked.

"Nothing. There's something I've been meaning to talk to you about."

Blair gave him a sideways glance. If they hadn't made love the way they did last night, she'd be worried about a 'talk.' Instead, she sat up and put her hands in her lap. "What do you want to talk about?"

"I've thought about this a lot. When you walked out, I thought I'd never see you again and

that scared me. I went to look for you, but I couldn't find you."

"I was nabbed by—"

"It doesn't matter. The fact of the matter is I thought I lost you forever. When I got off the plane yesterday and found you in the hospital, I knew I had a second chance. I wasn't going to

blow it this time."

"Blow what?"

"Blair Benson..." He knelt on one knee taking her left hand into his.

Blair put her other hand to her mouth and gasped. Her eyes welled with tears, and she

rocked back and forth.

"...will you marry me?" He reached into his pocket and pulled out a large diamond ring.

Blair couldn't speak. She nodded ecstatically. Lester put the ring on her finger, and she jumped him again. They fell to the floor, and without words she let him know how happy she

was.

* * *

"Blair... Get up, honey. We have to get going." He nudged her and tapped his watch. "It's

late."

Blair rolled over lazily and put her arm over Lester. "Just a little while longer. I'm so tired." Between the situation in Kansas City and the recent engagement, she had little time to catch her

breath. Lester slid out from under her arm and started to get dressed.

"Blair, we need to go, now. You can sleep in the car."

"Okay, I'm awake." She sat up and stared at her hand for a while. The sight of the ring was almost hypnotic. She put her clothes on.

After taking care of things at the front desk, the two walked to the car. While Blair was ecstatic about her engagement, she couldn't help but feel a bit off. Eddie was gone, and no one

knew where he was.

"We need to tell Eddie about this," she said.

"We will, once he resurfaces. Then we'll all celebrate."

Blair watched out her window as they sped down the interstate. She wrestled with her thoughts of happiness and worry. Hopefully, by the time she and Lester returned to Philly, they'd hear some news about Eddie.

CHAPTER NINETEEN

Z ealot made his way back to the farmhouse. With all his out-bursts and tantrums, the integrity of the house had weakened. He walked through a hole in the living room wall and collapsed onto the floor. The blast from the super suit did a number on him. The wounds up and down his body were

worse than he first realized. He laid there and stared at the ceiling. Blood pooled around him.

"You going to make it?" Bruce asked, looking down at him.

Zealot raised his hand and blasted the ghost with his lightning. He knew it wouldn't do anything, but deep down he felt a little better. "I'll live. I have to. Only the champion can kill me." He got to his feet and steadied himself against a chair. His thoughts were a bit scattered. The loss of blood

made him lightheaded.

"You might want to—" The ghost faded in and out, then it was gone.

Zealot wrinkled his brow. "Probably the injury," he said to himself.

"—try cleaning those wounds." The ghost flickered for a second or two, then winked back out

again.

Zealot focused on the spot where Bruce disappeared, but the ghost didn't return. The pain was

getting worse. He tried to remain on his feet, but his knees buckled.

Then he blacked out.

* * *

He woke up with a warm, tingling sensation coming from the wounds. The feeling radiated out through the rest of his body. The living room seemed different. The floor he was lying on felt hard and cold. Almost like…

Zealot sat up and looked around. He was on the Thiar ship again. He touched his stomach— the wounds were gone, his suit repaired. He got up off the floor and moved around the empty room. "What's going on?" he demanded. "You will show yourself to me."

A low rumbling noise rose up. It became a loud thunder within seconds. Zealot put his hands over his ears, but the sound came from inside his head. He fell down, writhing in pain. His skull

vibrated. It was so bad he thought his head might explode.

"You have been repaired," said a voice. Was that coming from his head also? "You will defeat

the Eoch's champion for us. We will be victorious."

"What happened to me? I thought I was invulnerable." The noise in his head started to die

down a little, but it was still enough to keep him on the ground.

"No earth weapon can harm you. We will be victorious."

"Yes, yes, I heard that." The noise came back strong. Zealot's body seized up until the sound

softened.

"You are failing in your mission. You must find the champion and defeat him."

"I've been trying. He just up and disappeared." The rumbling in Zealot's head finally drifted off,

and he rose to his feet.

"We anticipated this scenario. We have taken measures to make sure you and the other meet."

"What measures would that be?"

"True, we have instilled in you a strong desire to seek out the champion. But we wanted to ensure a speedy search. The longer it takes you to seek and destroy the other, the more your mind will leave you."

"A little overkill, don't you think?" *Why in the hell would they do that to their champion?* As if on cue, the voice answered his unspoken question.

"We added this in the event the one we chose could not, or would not, fight for us. The longer you go without fulfilling what we require of you, the more feral you become. Until you are nothing more than a beast."

He suddenly grasped what was happening at the farmhouse. It was them messing with his mind.

Before he could ask if it was permanent, the voice answered.

"Once you defeat the champion, we will return your mind to you."

"Then send me back so I can finish this and be done with you," he said.

In the blink of an eye, he found himself in the dilapidated house. Bruce was in front of him again.

"That's gotta rub you the wrong way. Them turning you into a mindless brute," he said

"You were there?"

"I'm in your head, remember." The ghost's image started to fade in and out again. "I think the more mind they take, the less of me you'll see."

"After all the terrible plans you've come up with, that might not be so bad."

"I do have one more thought for you."

"I don't want to hear it. It's bad enough that a piece of my old life haunts me, but it never has

anything of value to say. Was I that stupid in my former life?"

"I get it. Things haven't gone as well as they could. But this is bound to bring the champion

out."

Zealot turned away.

His adviser materialized in front of him. "And this will play to your strengths."

"All right. What is it?"

"You should—"

Pain shot through Zealot's head, and the ghost vanished. He didn't know how much time he had until he lost all thought and reason. The idea of becoming little more than a rabid dog angered him. He searched around for the ghost, but it was gone.

"I should what?" His rage intensified, and he unleashed a torrent of lightning, bringing down the rest of the house. The barn, about 300 yards from the house, also started to burn. With this much fire and smoke, there was no way people wouldn't notice. Zealot walked out of the burning

house and looked around again for his ghost. It was nowhere to be seen.

Zealot took to the air and flew off. He didn't know what to do. He had no plan and no direction. He hated his other half, but at least it came up with ideas. He was a blunt instrument created by the Thiar for one purpose—to kill the Eoch's champion. He was thrown into this fight

blind, and it frustrated him. He needed to be aimed at the right target or else he would miss again.

Another spike of pain shot through his head, and he plummeted out of the sky toward a forest. He took down a few trees and hit the ground hard. Zealot sat up. He heard something in the distance. He couldn't place it at first, but it became clearer the longer he focused.

"So, what do you think of the plan? It's guaranteed to bring him out." His ghost was back.

"I didn't hear the plan. You faded out again."

"Really?" Bruce looked around at the current surroundings. "Where's the house?"

"Gone."

"It was just a matter of time until you blew it up."

"What's your plan, Bruce? Every minute I don't find him, I get more and more savage."

"And that's a bad thing?"

"It is if I can't think for myself."

"Okay. From the top. You need to find a high-profile city and lay waste to it. No more hostages.

No more trying to lure the champion out. Just attack. Use that savagery to your advantage. The Thiar said no normal weapon could harm you. Let the world see what their new god can do when he gets angry."

"And if the ones with the alien tech show up again?"

"You'll tear them up too. Nothing fancy. No showboating. Just raw, unfiltered hate and death.

And when the other guy does show, you'll fly right into him. Your rage will be your weapon."

The idea sounded like it could work. But choosing the right city was the real gamble. He didn't

want to wait too long to go after him but didn't want to pick the wrong target.

The ghost snapped its fingers. "I got it. We'll go to the one spot in the country that he'll have to

come get you. There's no way he'd let you raze this city."

"Where?"

"Washington, D.C."

The thought was pure genius. The champion would never let Washington burn. He'd show up, and Zealot would finish the fight. Kill the champion, get his mind back, and from there he'd do

whatever he wanted. He might set himself up as a king.

"We should go as soon as possible. I don't know how fast my mind's degrading." Zealot

glanced around, but the ghost was gone.

It didn't matter. He had a target to aim for, and he'd hit it with everything he had.

CHAPTER TWENTY

H R sat in her office and poured over all the data that was collected during the incident in Kansas City. A detailed list of damaged and destroyed vehicles, weapons, and an unfortunate list of agents who were injured or dead. She was waiting on a report from her media team to see to what extent they were compromised. There was no way they could have remained completely covert. Her hope was that there was enough to construct an alibi with plausible deniability to keep the agency hidden. The encounter with Zealot in such a public place was a first for her and her team. Most confrontations were done out of sight of civilians or, at the very least, in an area they could contain

and control all the variables.

This fight left her feeling exposed. She wouldn't know the extent of it until the report was finished. Until then, she'd work on condolence letters to family members of the fallen agents. Their families never knew about their true job. Each one had a cover story they were required to memorize when they joined Cloak or Dagger. HR was thankful at times like these that she had no family. All of her immediate family already passed away and any extended relatives were so far down the family tree, none of them knew of her existence. The phone rang and jolted her out of the focused state she was in.

"HR, this is Agent Smith. You need to come see this." HR did not like the tone. It sounded like her worst fears were about to be confirmed. The call came from the main conference room down the hall.

When she got there, Agent Baker—Head of the Media Division—was at the end of the long conference table. A large monitor was on the wall with a still shot of Zealot and Agent Jones mid-flight.

"Where did this come from?" she asked and seated herself at the other end of the table.

"One of the news affiliates in Kansas City. It was picked up by all the networks and has been playing nonstop for hours." Around the table were other high-ranking members from both Cloak and Dagger.

"Is this all there is?"

"Not remotely. They have quite a bit of video. Both from the news and amateur video shot by people off their phones."

"How much is 'quite a bit'?" HR felt her stomach sink when Baker started the video from the beginning. It showed Zealot's attack on the agents and him destroying the market. Agent Jones could be seen fighting him. The worst of it was when Eddie came into the picture. His face displayed clear as day. There was no way they could run interference for him now. He was on his own. HR's new focus was on keeping her agents and the agency from any kind of blow back—from the press or, more importantly, the president. As if he heard her thoughts, a video call came in over the monitor.

"HR, what is going on?" The president didn't look pleased.

"Sir, I can assure you I have my best people on point. We'll make sure this gets contained. In a

day or two, all will be forgotten."

"There's no way this can be contained. The heads of the FBI, NSA, CIA, and every branch of

the military are calling me. They want to know if we're under attack from aliens."

"That's absurd, sir. They're not aliens."

"They're not? They certainly look like aliens, especially that Zealot guy."

"He and another individual were abducted by aliens and altered so they could take part in a

contest."

"A contest? Do you know how crazy this sounds? And I'm aware of your agency and all the things you have done. This still sounds nuts. If you don't fix this, I will have to take measures I don't

want to."

"I understand, Mr. President."

"For your sake, I hope you do." The screen went black.

HR looked around the room. Her agents were busily talking amongst themselves and jotting

down notes.

"Ideas," she said. "Anything you have. Give it to me."

The room got quiet. Eyes darted back and forth. No one wanted to look HR in the face. "Ma'am, we have nothing," a Dagger agent said.

"We've never had to deal with anything of this magnitude before," Smith said. "We're in

uncharted territory."

"I know." HR stood up and started to walk around the table. "In all my years, we've never let

something like this get this far out of control."

"What about Mr. Solomon? He could do a press conference and explain to the public that

there's nothing to worry about."

"Eddie Solomon is gone," HR said. "And we don't know where he is. And even if we did, he

wouldn't help us right now."

The men and women around the table exchanged glances, hoping someone would come up

with a plan, but no one did.

"This is going to destroy us," HR said. "The president will shut us down if we don't come up

with a plan to get people's minds off aliens and flying men."

"Why don't we just tell them?" Agent Baker said.

Everyone's head whipped around to the front of the room where he stood.

"Tell them? Tell who?" someone asked.

"The people. About us," he said.

"Are you mad? What kind of idiotic plan is that?" one of the agents said.

"Wait. Let's hear him out," HR said

"Thank you. What if we got out in front of this? We could give some of our less confidential findings to the press, and you could do an interview with someone from the White House." Baker

sat down and started to write something.

"We'd be exposing ourselves," Smith said.

"Only a little bit. We'd give them a watered-down version of what we do and how long we've been around. We tell the public just enough to get them over the shock of what's happened. After a

while, we'll be just another alphabet agency that no one will give a thought about."

HR sat down again. She had a lot to think about. If the nature of the agency was revealed, even a little, there could be disastrous consequences—and not just with HR and Cloak-Dagger. A great deal of the world's technology came from reverse engineering the alien devices that they acquired. Great lengths were made to slowly, and quietly, integrate the tech into society. They even disguised defensive weapons—using cover stories about cell phone towers or telescopic satellites—and placed them around the world. No one blinked an eye.

"Thank you very much, ladies and gentlemen. I have a lot to think about. You'll hear from me
shortly."

The agents filed out one by one and left HR alone. She replayed the video from the newsfeed a few more times. She paused it over and over to see if there was anything she could turn to her advantage. But there was nothing. Giving the world even a glimpse into what they've been doing felt like surrender. HR was not comfortable with that. She leaned back and closed her eyes.

Her mind drifted back to when she joined the organization, how proud she was to be able to help her country when other avenues weren't available. She remembered meeting the president for the first time, her partners over the years, and how she steadily rose through the ranks to Head of the Cloak and Dagger Division. It wasn't always easy, but she never gave up. And she didn't want to now.

HR walked back to her office and pulled a bottle of Captain Morgan from the bottom desk drawer. She pressed a button on her desk to lock down her office and turned on some music. She
made it through three quarters of a bottle, then reality set in.
There was no other option.

She had to reveal Cloak and Dagger and tell the public that they weren't alone in the universe. She didn't know how people would take the news, but that wasn't her problem. Leave that to the politicians to figure out. HR put the bottle back in the drawer and took out her tablet. A monitor came down from the ceiling with the Cloak-Dagger emblem on the screen. Another few taps and the president appeared on screen.

"President Edwards, I've made a decision on the incident." She sat as straight as possible and

crossed her arms in front of her on the desk.

"I'm surprised you made it this soon. I thought for sure you'd deliberate for a few days."

"Not necessary, sir. My team and I looked at all the options available to us, and I chose the one I thought was best." She hoped he couldn't see her bloodshot eyes. She was feeling the effects of her time with the Captain and made sure to enunciate every word so not to slur them. This would be

a bad time for the Commander in Chief to see her drunk.

"I'll be the judge of what is best," he said. "What is it?"

"Sir, I would like to sit down with you personally to discuss our plans. Even on a system as secure as this, I'd prefer a face to face."

HR heard other people in the background. There was no doubt his advisers were weighing in.

After a short pause, the president turned back toward the camera. "That's fine. But you'll be speaking to more than just me. I've already briefed the heads of the other agencies on your little

adventure. I'll invite them to the meeting. We'll all talk this through and come to an understanding."

HR clenched her teeth. "That's fine. When do you want to do this?"

"Get you and your team on the next flight to Washington. The sooner we can get this thing

under control and off the people's minds, the better."

"Very well, sir. See you soon." HR tapped the 'end call' button and the screen rescinded back up into the ceiling. She needed some time to get her hands on everything required to make her case,

including the people she wanted with her. She planned her arrival in D.C for the next evening.

She pulled up the phone on her tablet, highlighted five contacts, and pressed the 'conference call' button. "Agents, this is HR. Pack a bag and meet me in the hanger tomorrow afternoon. I'll

explain on the plane what's happening." She hung up.

She had a lot of work ahead of her, but for now she needed to finish some old business. The bottle clanked back onto the desk, and she poured herself another drink. This might be her last chance to enjoy some peace and quiet for a while.

CHAPTER TWENTY-ONE

Officer Lopez stood behind the yellow police tape. On the other side, there was the normal crowd that always showed up at a crime scene—nosey locals, people that liked to get on camera, and the random onlooker. Three different news vans each with their own cameraman and reporter were gearing up. For safety reasons the roadblock was a mile away from the actual scene. The crowd was relatively well behaved, and Lopez was happy for that. There had been too many times where the

crowd turned into a semi-contained riot.

"I thought you would have made detective by now."

Lopez turned to see who was behind the tape that shouldn't be. "Show yourself." He pulled out

a Taser and moved toward the voice. A figure walked out from around the corner of a building.

"Good to see you again, buddy." The man stood under a streetlight.

"Solomon? Is that you?" Lopez took a step back. The guy looked like Eddie, but he was quite bigger. Not what he remembered. Lopez had joined the LAPD a few years after Eddie. They were partnered up and became fast friends. He tried to contact Eddie after he left but never heard anything back. "What happened to you? Steroids?"

"It's a long story. What's going on here?" Eddie said.

"Wait, I haven't seen or heard from you in years, and you show up out of the blue looking like a... giant, and that's all you can say?"

Eddie took in a breath. "Quick version, I was hit with an alien beam that rewrote my DNA.

Now I have superpowers. Life has been... challenging."

"Wait, that was you in Kansas City, fighting that Zealot guy?"

"Yep. Wasn't much of a fight though."

"What are you doing here?"

"I needed to clear my head. I have some issues to work out."

"Well, it's good to see you again." He walked over and shook his hand. "There's a couple of morons held up in a convenience store nine blocks down. We have them pinned, but they're

determined to go out fighting."

"I could lend a hand."

"Yeah. You go on down there. Bradford would love to see you," Lopez said with a smirk. Detective Theo Bradford did not like Eddie. Bradford was a by-the-book guy, while Eddie flew by

the seat of his pants. As long as they did their jobs, no one cared. Still, Bradford resented him.

"Hey, Lopez. Good seeing you again."

"You too, Solomon."

Eddie turned and took off in a cloud of dust.

* * *

Eddie stood back and watched as the police tried to convince the shooters to walk out without sending in the swat team. Old memories came flooding back. All the times he was able to disarm a situation without loss of life. The way he felt when he was able to help someone in trouble. With the powers he had now, he could easily stop this and get everyone home safe. He walked up to Bradford and the officers with him.

"Long time, Theo," Eddie said.

"Who in god's name is at my crime scene?" he said and turned around to face Eddie. He

stretched his neck to look him in the eyes. "Solomon? What are you doing here?"

"Came to lend a hand."

"Are you still part of the LAPD?"

"No."

"Then get out." Bradford had what Eddie called a 'Napoleon complex.' He was a small guy with a big guy attitude. Eddie took a step forward and everyone stepped back, except Bradford. He

stepped toward Eddie and stuck his finger in his chest. "This has nothing to do with you so beat it."

"I can help. I have—"

Bradford turned his back to Eddie and walked to his car. "I know all about what you can do. I watch the news. You screwed the pooch in KC. Well, I'm not going to let you screw things up here.

So go."

One of the officers came up to Bradford. "He might be able to—"

"If the next word out of your face is 'help,' I'll see to it you hand out parking tickets for the rest

of your life."

"Come on, Theo. That's a bit much, isn't it?" Eddie said.

"It's Detective Bradford to you, Solomon. Now go before I arrest you."

"I know when I'm not wanted." Eddie walked past Bradford and the others, past the cars, and

straight for the store.

"Where do you think you're going?" Bradford yelled.

"You don't want to talk. Fine, I'll go talk to them." He heard the distinctive sound of a gun being drawn. He stopped and turned around.

"I will shoot you."

"I fell from space a few days ago. Hurt like hell. I don't know if I'm bullet proof, but I'll take the risk, so you do what you think you have to do." Eddie turned and continued to the convenience store.

Bradford yelled obscenities and kicked the squad car. Eddie heard him holster his gun.

At the front of the store, the lights were out and shelving pushed in front of the window and door to barricade it. He heard people talking but couldn't make out the words.

He peeked through a crack in the window. "Anybody home?"

Gunfire erupted from inside the store. Eddie turned to check on the officers. They were behind their cars, and no one was hurt. He heard movement now. It sounded like they were moving to the back of the store.

"The only way this gets resolved is if you give yourselves up. Peacefully."

More shots were fired. One hit Eddie in the arm. He examined his arm for damage. There was none. The bullet stung where it hit, but nothing penetrated the skin.

He smiled and turned toward the blockade. "Bradford, I am bulletproof." Bradford gave him the finger and walked away.

Eddie walked to the doors and pulled them off their hinges. He kicked the shelves across the floor and stepped inside. "I'm coming in," he announced. "If I were you, I'd give up."

Two guys jumped out from behind some shelves and shot at him. One of them brandished a shotgun, while the other held a handgun. Every bullet hit him and clanked to the ground.

With a quickness, he moved on the shooter holding the pistol. He grabbed the gun and delivered a palm strike, sending the shooter into the wall. The other guy dropped the shotgun and made a break for the back door. Eddie ran up behind him and grabbed him by his jacket. The guy kept running, but his feet weren't on the ground. Eddie tossed him back into the store.

"What are you?" asked the gunman. He crawled backward as Eddie walked over to him.

"Just a guy trying to make sure everyone gets out of this alive." He picked him up again and

dangled him like a stray dog.

The shooter punched him and yelped, then pulled his hand back. "I think it's broken, man." His

hand hung limp.

Eddie grabbed the other shooter and threw him over his shoulder. "Don't shoot," he yelled.

"We're coming out!" He walked out of the store and dropped the two onto the cement.

Five officers swarmed them. They laid them on their stomachs and cuffed their hands behind their backs. While one officer Mirandized the thieves, Bradford came from around the cars and ran

up to Eddie.

"Do you know what you've done?" He wrung his hands.

"Yeah, stopped bad guys," Eddie said and shrugged.

"And what happens if they say we used excessive force? One guy has a broken hand and the

other still isn't conscious."

"That guy could have broken his hand on anything."

"But he didn't. Now we're going to have to deal with the fallout while you walk away. Again."

Eddie winced. After his wife's death, Eddie didn't even stop to clean out his locker or pick up his belongings. He called his captain and quit. This left a bad taste in the mouths of a lot of people

on the force. Bradford already didn't like him, and now he had even more reason to.

"There's no pleasing you, is there?" Eddie walked over to Bradford and pushed one of the cars

aside to get to him.

The officers drew their weapons.

"You going to hit me, Solomon?" Bradford stuck out his chin.

Eddie stood there and stared at Bradford. With everything that's happened, his nerves were

shot and right now his tolerance for Bradford's attitude was at a zero.

"You were always a weasel, Theo—making everyone's life hell so you could look good. If I did

hit you, you'd deserve it."

Bradford took a step back and put his hands up, ready to fight.

"I want nothing to do with you," Eddie said. He turned and started to walk away.

"Once a coward, always a coward. Right, Solomon?"

Eddie moved so fast that no one saw him turn around and grab Bradford. He picked him up and looked him in the eyes. "You have no idea what I've been through." His eyes glowed brighter than normal. His hands trembled. He could drive this weasel into the ground, and no one could stop him. Instead, he opened his hands and let Bradford fall to the ground. "If you see me again, walk the

other way. I might not be as forgiving."

Eddie leapt into the air and flew away.

He closed his eyes. *I can't believe the way I acted back there.* True, he was under a lot of pressure, but that's no reason to act the way he did. When this alien business was behind him, he'd come back and apologize. And he needed to ask forgiveness from Blair too. Leaving her in Kansas City all alone

with HR was irresponsible. After all, he was the one that allowed her to get dragged into this mess.

A buzzing came from his pocket. It was a text from Blair:

I'm fine, in case you're wondering. Back in Philly with Lester.

He let out a sigh of relief. Now he just needed to get home and make amends, then finish this fight with Zealot. There was no way his life could get back to normal until that was done. He slid the phone back into his pocket and flew home with lightning speed.

CHAPTER TWENTY-TWO

Lester watched the sun come up over the city as he pulled up to his apartment. The drive from Kansas City was more tiring than he expected. Blair was sound asleep in the back seat.

He reached behind him and gave her arm a shake. "We're home, sleepyhead."

She made some grumbling noises and swatted at Lester. "Just five more minutes."

"Come on. I need to return this to the rental place, and I'm sure they won't take it with you sleeping in the back."

"All right. Okay, I'm up." Blair sat up and rubbed her eyes. "I thought you were going to drop me off at my place."

"We've had a long drive. I thought we'd just come back here for a while."

"There were some things I wanted to do today."

"You can still do them. Come up, and you can go back to sleep. I'll clean up and take the car back. Then we'll do whatever you want."

Blair leaned forward and gave Lester a kiss. "Fine. I'll make some coffee."

Lester opened the apartment door, and Blair gasped in surprise.

He watched her roam around the living room. He had set up her collection of ceramic bells on the mantel and placed her lamp next to his couch. Her pictures hung on the walls. He even stacked up some of her comic books on the coffee table.

"Lester, what's going on?" She walked around the room in shock. She moved to the kitchen.

"You brought my whole kitchen."

"I used the spare key. I wanted to move some of your things here and get a jump start on our new life."

"And the rest of my things?"

"I had them put in storage. We can decide how we want to integrate our two apartments into one later. Are you surprised?" He had a childlike grin.

Blair walked back into the living room and sat down on the couch. "It's great," she said although her tone conveyed something less than great. "But don't you think I should have had a say in this?"

"It would have ruined the surprise."

"And if I would have said no, then what?"

"Luckily, we don't have to worry about that. You're here now, and we can plan for what's next."

"Okay. What's next?"

Lester could tell she was annoyed with his home make-over. He knew once the shock wore off, she'd be grateful for his bold actions. He sat down and wrapped his arms around her. She put her head on his shoulder. "Next, we talk marriage details. Nothing specific. Just generally what you want."

"Well, I'd like a small ceremony. I don't have any family to speak of, and you have Eddie. Oh,

speaking of Eddie..."

"Yes?" Lester's voice dripped with disdain. He didn't even try to hide it.

"What's that all about? I just wanted to tell you I sent him a text."

"Did he text you back?"

"Not yet."

Good. Eddie had to butt into everything, didn't he?

Lester smiled. "Blair, I know we're the only two people in your life. You find it hard to connect

with others. But can we have one conversation without you bringing up my brother?"

"I just thought since he's—"

"He's what, Blair?"

"He's—"

Lester cut her off before she could finish her thought. "We're here to talk about our life together. We're getting married. Eddie is my brother, and I know you look up to him, but you are

the focus of my life right now."

"If we are going to start a family, then we need to include the whole family. Neither of us have much of an extended family. I have none to be exact. And besides a couple of uncles and an aunt

that you never hear from, Eddie is all you have."

"It just seems like we can't go one hour without bringing up Eddie. 'Where's Eddie?' 'Is Eddie

coming by today?' 'Let's call Eddie and see if he wants to come along.'"

"My family was cold and distant. They couldn't have cared less about how I was doing. I was more of a guest in our house than a daughter. They missed more of my birthdays than a family should. With my dad away for business and my mom with her friends, I had to fend for myself." "I'm sorry you had that kind of childhood."

"I always promised myself that if I started my own family, I'd make sure no one's forgotten.

That included my future husband's family as well."

"You know the history I have with Eddie."

"Yeah, and I thought you were working on fixing it."

Lester got up and paced around the living room. All he wanted to do was plan the rest of their lives out. He didn't want to open this can of worms. But if Blair was going to insist on dragging Eddie's name into every part of his life, then he had no choice but to tell her exactly how he felt.

"To be completely honest Blair, I never wanted to fix things." Lester paced even faster.

"What do you mean?" She shook her head.

"When Eddie came back from California, he was a broken man. I didn't know what brought him back. But I didn't care. I just saw an opportunity to get something over on him—to put him

under my thumb the way he had me."

"I can't believe what I'm hearing. That's terrible. He was in pain, and you used that to make

yourself feel better? Eddie's been nothing but good to us."

"He never cared for our family. He always took and took. Our dad gave him everything, and he threw it in his face and left. When he came back, I saw my chance to get even. Give him just enough

to help him get by but keep him dependent on me."

Blair's eyes weld up and tears rolled down her face. "How can you be so narcissistic? Is that how you're going to treat me? Our children? Things to control so you can feel better about

yourself?" She pulled some tissues from her purse and wiped her eyes.

"No, I love you. I would never do that."

"Yet you can kick your own flesh and blood when he's down." Blair began to sob. "You're crushing me, you know? How could you mistreat another person like that, let alone your own

brother?"

"Blair, I didn't want to go down this road today," he groaned. "I want to talk about our future and the life we're going to make together."

Blair slowed her breathing and composed herself. "Lester, if you want to salvage this and get us back on track, then you're going to need to make things right with Eddie. Whatever happened in the

past is in the past."

"You don't understand—"

"Oh, I understand more that you think I do. Family is important to me. And if we're going to make this work, then family needs to be important to you too. No more excuses. If and when Eddie gets back—"

"More 'if' than 'when,'" he said. Blair's eyes narrowed in anger. He put his hands up and took a

step back.

"When Eddie gets back"—her voice turned sharp and demanding—"you are going to make an

extensive effort to work with him and make things right."

"And if I refuse, are you going to walk out again?" Lester regretted his words as soon as they left his lips. He sat down next to Blair and took her hands and held them. "I'm sorry. I didn't mean

it like that."

She pulled away from him and wiped her eyes again. "Lester Eugene Solomon, we're going to

need some work if you want us to get married. There's more to life than you and what you want."

"I know. I'm sorry. I'll do whatever I need to do to make this work. I want us to have the kind

of family we've always wanted."

"Then make things right with Eddie."

The contempt he had for his brother was strong. He hid it well enough, but he wasn't sure if he could overcome it, even for Blair. He'd try though. "How should I do that?" He really had no idea.

He let his anger dictate his actions for years. Could he just put that aside now?

"Start by listening to him and being supportive. It can go a long way in helping you get over the resentment you have for him." Blair clasped her hands together and lifted them to her mouth, as if she was hoping against hope Lester would listen to her words. "Lester, I love you. Please try. For

me."

Lester held his arms out. Blair hesitated for a moment and then leaned in for the hug. The things he said could be forgiven, but he knew Blair wouldn't easily forget them. She laid her head on his shoulder and let out a little sigh.

Out of nowhere, the living room shook and the windows rattled. They both jumped to their feet and steadied the fragile items that were shifting around the room. Lester couldn't even

remember the last time an earthquake hit Philadelphia. It seemed unlikely that's what it was now.

As if reading each other's minds, they exchanged glances and shared the same thought aloud.

"Eddie."

The front door opened and in walked Eddie. His clothes were shredded. With one motion, he put his arms around them and picked them up into a bear hug. "I have missed you guys so much,"

he said. He gave both Lester and Blair a kiss on the cheek and let them down.

"Wow, Eddie. Are you all right?" Lester said.

"I am now. I have so much to talk to you two about. So much to apologize for." Eddie sat down in the recliner and leaned back. "I'm exhausted. It takes a lot of energy to fly from California nonstop."

"You went to California? Okay." Blair folded her arms and crossed her legs.

"You have every right to be mad at me. But while I was there, I met a guy that helped me see

what was going on my life. I'm back on track."

"Well, you can tell us everything over breakfast," Blair said. "You buy this time." She gave

Lester a jab with her elbow.

"Yes, we want to hear everything," Lester said.

"Great. Let's go. You'll love this. We going to our usual place?"

"Of course," Lester said. "They make the best pancakes and bacon."

"I have to go and grab some clothes. I'll meet you there."

The three of them left the apartment. Lester and Blair took the car, and Eddie jumped into the air. Blair stared off into the sky for a few moments. Then she looked at Lester. He knew without a word what she was thinking.

He smiled at her. "I'm turning over a new leaf today. Guaranteed."

CHAPTER TWENTY-THREE

It had only been a few hours, but Zealot's mind had degraded to an almost animal-like state. There was pain in his head and a ringing in his ears like he heard on the Thiar ship. He still had enough of himself, whoever that really was, to remember the plan. The problem now was

executing it.

He ran through the wooded area. Every now and then he stopped and looked around.

"I need to... think—no, remember... Washington." Whatever happened—no matter what—he must remember that. Washington was his destination. Nothing could keep him from

that.

Something caught his attention from the corner of his eye—the ghost. He needed to talk to Bruce. He ran over, but it was gone. Up ahead he saw it again. He ran faster this time, hoping to

catch it. Gone again. The beast in him became enraged. This was a game he did not want to play.

Zealot heard noises. He couldn't recognize them, but maybe they could tell him where the ghost was. He ran to the edge of a small cliff and lights shone into his eyes. Some white, some red, traveling in opposite directions. They were loud, and the noise made his head hurt worse. He covered his ears, but it was useless. The sounds were familiar. He inched his way closer to the edge and tried to recall where he'd heard them before. The ground gave way under him, and

he fell off the cliff and hit the road. He bounced once, then rolled across the median strip.

The white lights coming at him swerved away to avoid hitting him. The red ones kept going. Zealot yelled something unintelligible. Between the ringing in his ears and the noise the lights made, he couldn't hear himself. A group of white lights headed in his direction. It let out a noise so loud it cut right through the others. Zealot ran toward it.

A burnt smell caught his attention as the lights slowed to a screeching halt. He ran to them and slashed with his claws. The lights went out, but something sprayed him. The smell was terrible. He shielded his face from it. The lights were connected to a metal box. Zealot grabbed it and swung it at the other lights. More screeching sounds followed with even more burning

smells. Everything he did to make the noises stop just caused more horrid sounds.

Zealot became more and more agitated, then he saw Bruce ahead of him. The ghost was trying to say something, but Zealot was too far away to hear it. He jumped over the metal barrier, and the lights divided. The red lights passed right through Bruce as if they didn't see the ghost. The lights were about to catch up to Zealot, so he turned and struck out at them. They

went flying to the side and hit other lights. He looked back, and the ghost was gone again.

"Where are you?" he screamed. "Why do you run?"

Now shattering noises rang out along with the others. His entire field of vision blurred with red and white lights. Did he hear people yelling? He didn't know if the screams were real or all in his head. He threw lightning at everything around him in a blind rage. Explosions rocked the

area, and the heat from them felt good on his face. Fire meant he was winning against the lights.

From the other side of where the lights were, he saw the ghost. Bruce was up on a hill surrounded by more trees. Zealot didn't like chasing his ghost. It normally showed up next to him, or at least that's what he thought it used to do. He launched himself up over the tangle of

lights to the hill where Bruce stood.

"Stop running. I need... answers," he cried.

More trees. More hide and seek. He let more lightning loose, and trees burst into flames. Some of the trees ruptured from the intense heat of the lightning, and Zealot was hit by pieces

of wood and dirt.

"I will find you!"

Through the smoke and flames, he saw the ghost. It stood there, as if waiting for him. Zealot shuffled past the fire and debris and found himself in a small clearing with the ghost a short distance away. He walked up with caution. He didn't want it to disappear again. It simply

stood its ground until Zealot was close enough to touch it.

"Why are you running?" he said.

"I'm not. Your mind is pushing us apart."

"I don't—I don't... know what... what..." He knew what he wanted to say, but he had

trouble forming the thoughts. He slapped himself on the head in the hope it might jump start

something.

"Don't hit yourself. It won't help anything," Bruce said.

Zealot tried again to speak. A word or two came out, but the rest was senseless babble.

The ghost held up its hands. "Stop. I don't have much time left. The part of your mind that—" The ghost blinked out and back again behind him. Zealot spun around. "—I'm in is deteriorating. If you ever want to get your mind back—" Again, it disappeared and reappeared off to his right. "—you need to get to Washington, D.C. Whatever happens, that's the one thing

you cannot forget."

Zealot snorted and looked around. The sun came up over the horizon.

The ghost pointed in the direction of the sunrise. "That way. Go that way. Look for a big white house with a dome on top. That's where—" The ghost vanished. Zealot spun around, but

it was gone. No more help. He was on his own.

Loud piercing sounds with red and blue lights came closer and closer. Zealot didn't want to be around when they showed up. He glanced toward the east, where the sun was just over the hills, and ran in that direction. He wasn't about to let anything stop him from completing his

mission.

With his last bit of humanity, he yelled out one word: "Wash...ing...ton!" He'd get his mind back or die trying.

CHAPTER TWENTY-FOUR

The plane ride to Washington took longer than normal. HR had the pilot swing out far over the Atlantic. Since the exposure of her organization, she wanted to be as careful as possible. Concealing the location of their compound was a top priority. If anyone found the alien technology that was stored in the warehouse, there's no telling what damage could be done. And if another government agency were to possess it, that damage would be magnified by one hundred.

She never met the current president in person. Since he took office, they had only spoken over the secured line in her office. Traveling to meetings like this was unheard of. Her focus was always on the smooth operation of Cloak-Dagger.

"We'll be arriving in Washington, D.C. in approximately ten minutes."

The announcement snapped HR out of her trance. She'd been studying every file she had on the agency chiefs and those around them. Every detail mattered. She wasn't going into this blind. After she packed up the files and put them in her briefcase, she stood up and turned around. The agents she brought with her stopped what they were doing and gave her their attention.

"I know this seems crazy to some of you; it seems like that to me. But I assure you, I have this situation under control." Since the events in Kansas City, everyone in Cloak-Dagger were on edge. They dedicated their lives to preserving the secrecy of their mission. Now with them being outed, they looked to HR for guidance. She planned to do everything in her power to see that the organization continued.

"I know we've talked about this, but what if they suggest shutting us down?" Smith asked.

HR walked down the aisle and took a seat next to him. "It won't come to that. We have a lot to bargain with. We have information they want. Plus, aliens will always visit us, and we're the best option they have to keep the peace." HR wanted to believe what she said. But she had no idea what to expect when they got there. As far as she knew, they could very well dismantle Cloak-Dagger and reassign—or retire—everyone in the organization.

"Please fasten your seat belts. We're making our final approach for Washington, D.C. now."

* * *

A fleet of cars waited for them on the tarmac. HR took a deep breath and mentally prepared herself for a fight.

The agents were shown to one car, while HR was escorted to a different one. Once inside she saw the president was there.

She sat down across from him and extended her hand. "It's a pleasure to finally meet you in person, Mr. President." She liked the fact that he had a firm handshake. The last president had a limp-wristed shake. She hated that and did whatever she could to not have to shake his hand.

"Likewise. I probably don't have to say it, but there are some upset people at the White House

that can't wait to grill you over this."

"I'm not worried. I've dealt with hostile alien warlords. These guys are going to be easy."

The president shook his head and chuckled. "HR, I'm aware of all that you and your team have

done for not just our country but for the world. I'll do everything I can to back you up."

"Thank you, sir. I appreciate it. But I'll warn you now, if they try to force you to shut us down,

then there will be trouble."

"Don't worry. I'm sure it won't come to that." The president's phone rang. He turned away from HR. She tried not to listen in on his conversation and went back to preparing herself for the

questions. After a few minutes, he hung up and continued his briefing with her.

"We're going to take you and your people to the hotel. You can rest, and tomorrow morning we'll pick this up and get everything squared away."

"That would be great. We've all been under a lot of stress lately. A bit of rest sounds wonderful." HR didn't want rest. She barely slept on good days. HR wanted to get this over with as soon as possible. She leaned back in her seat. At least this would give her a few more hours to

prepare her case and plan for anything out of the ordinary.

The hotel was not what she expected. HR thought that they might have been dropped off

in the wrong part of town. She went to the front desk to check in. "Excuse me, ma'am. I'm—"

"You and your team are already checked in," the desk clerk said and then handed HR several keys attached to large plastic circles with room numbers printed on them. She took the keys and walked back to the agents.

"Is this how they treat all their guests?" asked Agent Baker.

"I have a feeling they don't want us near the city, in case we run into anyone we'll talk to

tomorrow," HR said.

"Still"—Agent Smith motioned to the lobby—"it seems a bit... shady?" The clerk looked

up at him, and he flashed her a smile. She smiled back and continued with her work.

"We're not here on vacation," HR snapped at the group. "We'll go to our rooms, clean up,

and get a good night's rest. I'll call everyone in the morning so we can get our things and go."

The agents all nodded in unison and went to their rooms.

HR understood their frustration. Normally, she would have been put up in a five-star hotel, and this was about four stars below that. Was someone sending her a message? This would be dealt with tomorrow. She made her way to the elevator and tried to take her own advice before

the 'inquisition.'

* * *

It seemed like she just closed her eyes when the alarm on her phone went off. HR rolled over and checked the time. It was seven o'clock. She got up and got dressed. There was a coffee maker in the room, but it looked like it hadn't been used in some time. She called each member of her team and then made her way to the lobby. Before she could read a little of the

complementary newspaper, the agents were surrounding her.

"The sooner we leave, the better," Agent Baker said.

HR nodded. "They're sending cars to take us to breakfast, then to the White House. If

everything goes as planned, we'll be home by this evening."

As if on que, the driver walked in and let them know their ride was there. The team moved quickly out of the lobby and into the cars. For HR this day couldn't end soon enough. She just

wanted to get things straightened out and get back to work.

After breakfast and a nice ride through the city, they made their way to the White House and were directed to a large conference room. The seal of the president was on the back wall, and a portrait of him was on the opposite wall. HR took a seat with Agents Smith and Baker on either side of her. People from other agencies came in and took seats. Some held briefcases,

while others carried folders bursting with multicolored papers.

After waiting almost an hour, two secret service agents came in and gave the room a quick

sweep. "It's all clear. Send him in," one of them said.

Everyone stood as President Jason Edwards walked in. He took his seat at the head of the

table, and everyone else followed.

"Sorry for the delay," he said. "There was an incident last night that was brought to my

attention. HR, I think this is something you should see."

HR perked up. She wondered what was going on. A screen rose behind her, and she and her team turned around.

Video taken from a phone showed Zealot attacking cars on a highway. With the strange way he moved, HR thought he behaved more like an animal—not like he was in Kansas City.

Here, he flailed his arms and swatted at passing cars like they were flies.

"Can you tell us anything about this, HR?" the president asked.

She turned back around and opened a file folder with her notes. "No, sir. While this does

look like Zealot, his actions aren't what we've observed."

"You're 'observing' this nut? Why didn't you know about this then?" Spencer Jordan asked.

HR knew she was in a hostile environment. As the Head of the FBI, Jordan prided himself on being privy to even the most inconspicuous events. To find out a clandestine group was working in secret with the president's knowledge must have been a surprise to him and

everyone else at the table.

"We handle threats of alien incursion as discreetly as we can, but this particular one is a bit

more complicated."

"I don't think destroying downtown Kansas City counts as discreet." Jordan leaned back in

his chair.

"We have never dealt with this kind of being. Most of our interactions with aliens were peaceful. They came here to study and understand us. A few times there have been aliens with

more sinister motives, but we were able to deal with them without alarming the world at large."

"Then what makes this one different?" Robert Graham—Head of Homeland Security— spoke up. "Why cause all this damage? It's destroyed two different cities while calling out some 'champion.'"

"This situation is one we never thought of. We—"

"You never thought an alien might wage war on us? Come and blow up our cities and towns?" Jordan asked. "I thought that was your job."

"Zealot isn't interested in taking over our planet. He and another man were—"

"This Zealot monster is human?"

"He was before an alien race abducted him and altered him to fight. There are two alien races orbiting our plant. They each chose one person to act as their champion in a trial by combat. The winning side will destroy the loser and then go back to their own world. As far as

we know, neither side has any hostel intentions toward us."

"That's not very reassuring. What if this creature wins? Will he leave with the aliens?"

Jordan asked.

HR felt the tension in the room rise with each question asked. She had no solid answers for

them. Without giving up all their secrets, all she could do was pacify their concerns.

"While the events in Kansas City could have been handled differently, we are confident that we can assist the other champion and help him eliminate Zealot before any more damage is

done."

"You've been working with the other one? For how long?" Jordan yelled. He leapt out of his chair and leaned into HR's space. "How do we know the one you're working with won't turn on us if he wins? How can we be sure of anything? All we have is your word. And until a few days ago, we didn't even know you or your organization existed." "Spencer," the president said, "sit down. You're embarrassing yourself."

Jordan sat back down and took a deep breath.

The president continued, "Now, let's hear what HR has to say about the other altered

person and their interactions."

"Sir, there's not much to tell. We reached out to him as soon as we were made aware. Brought him in, and he agreed to help us. You've all seen the video of Kansas City. After that, he flew off. We haven't heard from him since." HR was fine giving them the short version of her dealings with Mr. Solomon. While his face was all over the news, his name had not yet been

made public. She wasn't going to be the one to out him.

The grilling went on for what seemed like hours. As HR looked around the room for any kind of escape, her tablet vibrated. She swiped the screen a few times. Just as she started to type something, eight secret service agents came into the room. They moved Jordan aside and

escorted the president from the room.

"What's going on?" Graham asked.

Everyone in the room reached for their phones.

HR took the opportunity to leave the room unnoticed, and her agents followed. She pulled

them aside.

"Zealot is here in D.C. He's destroying everything in his path. We need to mobilize Dagger

and slow him down until Mr. Solomon gets here."

"How do we know he'll show?" Smith asked.

"We don't."

CHAPTER TWENTY-FIVE

E ddie stood waiting in front of the diner as they drove into the parking lot. The Griddle Hut was the place to go for a real homemade breakfast—pancakes as big as the plate and a side of bacon

that took up a second plate. Lester and Blair walked around to the front.

Eddie held the door for them. "After you," he said.

Blair noticed his smile. It was genuine. As long as she'd known him, his smiles always looked forced or fake. Something he did to blend into normal society. But this smile—it had actual joy

behind it.

They made their way past the counter. People stopped eating and stared at the giant of a man walking past them. Eddie didn't seem bothered by it. They came to a table near the back and sat

down.

"You look happy," Blair said.

"I am happy. First time in a long time I feel good."

"So, this guy you talked to, he cured you of your depression?" Lester said. Blair swatted him on

the arm.

"No, I'm not cured. But I do have a different outlook on life."

Lester sat back. Cynicism came off him in waves. "Do tell. What words of wisdom turned you around?" Blair's jaw dropped. She was mad and embarrassed. Lester promised her he would change, and he was falling back on his word.

"Gratitude. I always looked at how terrible my life was and what I didn't have. Now when I feel myself slipping into my funk, I remind myself of everything I still have. I'm thankful for you and Blair. Without you guys, life would really be hard."

"We're thankful for you too," Blair said. She nudged Lester. "Tell Eddie how you feel about him."

The waitress came over and filled their coffee cups and took their orders.

Lester, still mulling over what to say, took a sip of his drink and looked at Eddie. "I feel like I don't matter whenever you're around." He took another sip and set his cup down.

"Lester!" Blair was shocked. They talked on the car ride over, and he promised her that he wouldn't start any trouble.

"What? I don't understand," Eddie said.

"Lester?" Blair nudged him again.

Lester kept his head down and stared at his coffee as he continued. "You always got the most attention when we were kids. Even after you left, Dad still thought more highly of you than me." When he finally looked up, his eyes were red with tears running down his face. His voice rose as he went on. "And when you came back home, broken and sad, I finally felt like I surpassed you. I had a great job. Someone who loves me. Everything was going my way. But the universe, in its infinite wisdom, has once again chosen to elevate you. You've disrupted my work, stolen my fiancée." He paused, then drank some more coffee.

The other patrons in the diner stopped eating and started to watch them.

"I didn't steal anything," Eddie said. "I'm sorry you feel this way, but I'm not the one to blame. I never wanted all the attention. I never wanted to follow Dad's 'plan' for my future. This is crazy talk."

"Lester, this isn't what I meant..." Blair couldn't believe her ears. Eddie knew his brother blamed him for all his troubles as a teenager, but Eddie always went out of his way to help Lester whenever he could since he came home. How could Lester think he didn't matter? Blair didn't know what to do. She loved Lester, but she didn't know the man who sat before her now. She wanted the two of them to repair their relationship, and he was destroying it.

"God help me, when that beam hit you, I hoped it was going to kill you." Lester let out a sigh and leaned forward. He looked Eddie right in the eyes. "I really thought when we dragged you home, it would be the last thing I'd have to do for you."

Blair, furious, got up and stormed toward the restroom.

* * *

Eddie sat there and didn't say a word. He was dumbfounded to hear what Lester really thought.

His brother leaned back and sipped his coffee. He glanced out of the window with a strange, satisfied smile on his face. It was almost as if a sense of peace overcame him. Eddie was visibly shaken, and Lester didn't seem to care. Eddie would never use his power to hurt his own blood, but after this truth bomb, he'd never trust Lester again.

Eddie fumbled through his pockets and pulled out his anxiety medication. He learned a lot about handling the attacks, but what Lester just told him was beyond anything he could have imagined. He popped two pills into his mouth and stood up.

"I don't know what's going on in your head," he said. "You're right. You have surpassed me, and I'm honestly thrilled by it. I hope you and Blair have a wonderful life together." Eddie put his hand on his brother's shoulder. Lester shrugged it off and went back to his coffee.

Eddie noticed everyone in the diner staring at them, and he decided it was a good time to make an exit. Just as he reached the door, the television at the front counter caught his attention. The volume was down, but he watched as Zealot launched his red lightning at the Washington monument.

"Can you please turn that up?" he asked the waitress.

One of the diners at the counter pointed at him. "That's right. You're that guy from Kansas City."

Eddie gave him a nod and went back to the TV. The headline across the bottom read 'Crazed Alien Attacks Nation's Capital.' The waitress gave Eddie the remote, and he turned up the sound to hear the reporter.

"We still have no idea what, if any, demands he has. What we do know is, as of now, the president and his cabinet have been moved to a secure location, and the military has been called in to contain the threat and help in evacuations." "They don't stand a chance against him," Eddie said.

The diners were still watching him.

"Shouldn't you go and stop him?" the waitress asked.

The others all nodded in agreement.

"Yeah, you need to go and stop that thing," another diner added.

Eddie looked back at the table Lester sat at. He was still drinking his coffee like nothing was wrong. Eddie reached into his pocket and pulled out some money. "Here. This is for their breakfast." He motioned toward his brother. "Keep the change". The waitress took the money, and

Eddie sped off.

* * *

Blair sat down across from Lester. She returned from the bathroom, still visibly angry. All eyes
were still on them.

Lester reached across the table and held Blair's hands. "Once we
get all our wedding plans in order, everything will be fine. You'll see."

Blair tilted her head. "Wedding plans?" She scoffed. "You just told
your brother you wished he was dead. You really think I'm going to
marry you now?" She pulled her hands away and got up
from her chair.

Lester grabbed her wrist as she walked past him. "Where are you
going?" he demanded.

Blair curled her lip. "To find Eddie and apologize for you. Then
I'm calling a mover to get my stuff out of your apartment. I think it's
best we don't see each other for a while. A long while." She
tried to pull her hand away, but he tightened his grip.

"We're building a life together. I love you." Lester's eyes told
another story.

"I don't know if you even know the meaning of the word 'love,'
Lester." She pulled harder this
time, and he let her go. Her wrist was red and in pain. She shook
her head and walked away.

Lester called out to her. "Eddie's gone. He's probably halfway to
Washington by now."

"What do you mean?"

"Check out what's on TV." Lester kept his back to her the entire
time. This hurt her as much as
him grabbing her wrist. She walked up to the front counter and
watched the news unfold.

"You know that guy that was here?" one of the diners asked.

"I do. He's my friend." She rubbed her wrist while she watched. "I
need to help him."

Lester jumped up from his chair. "There you go again," he shouted. He walked up to her and pointed at the screen. "You can't help yourself, can you? Eddie runs into danger, and you follow him like a puppy dog. It's sad how pathetic you've become. And you wonder why I hate Eddie so

much. I love you, but all you want to do is follow him. Fine, go after him. I'll even drive you."

"You'd drive me to Washington?"

"Yes. On the way there, maybe I can talk some sense into you."

"And maybe I can help you see where you're wrong. All this time Eddie was back, trying to repair your relationship, and you still held on to your hate."

"Let's go," Lester said. He walked past Blair and out the door.

Blair looked around, and her cheeks grew hot from embarrassment.

A woman sitting at the far end of the counter came over to her. "You can do better. He'll never

change," she said.

"I have to try. One more time." She gave the woman a hug and walked to the exit.

"Be careful," the woman shouted after her.

Blair turned around and gave her a wave. She realized what she must have looked like to them. A woman not strong enough to walk away from what was obviously a bad relationship. She hoped they were wrong. She wanted things to work out. Deep down, she had a feeling they wouldn't. But

another part of her, the stubborn part, kept hope alive.

Lester pulled the car around and beeped the horn. She ran around and got in.

The trip down was not going to be fun. If there was one thing Blair both loved and hated about Lester, it was the way he could argue. It helped him in the courtroom, but outside of it, it frustrated her to no end. Every time she tried to defend her position on a topic, he'd find ten things wrong. By

the time he was done, she'd rethink her stance and, more times than not, take Lester's side.

To her surprise he said nothing.

Lester stared straight ahead as if in a trance. This frightened her. The display at the diner was bad but complete silence—this was a new level of anger for him. Blair turned on her phone to look for updates about Zealot. She didn't know what to expect when they got to Washington, but she knew nothing would be the same when the dust settled.

CHAPTER
TWENTY-SIX

H R and her team ran onto the White House lawn. Her mobile command truck materialized through a green teleportation door. It rolled to a stop, and the door closed behind it. The crew made their way into the truck and sat down in various seats. HR stood and surveyed the scene from the bank of monitors along the wall. Several teams of Cloak agents had teleported in and were evacuating civilians and reinforcing high value targets. In her earpiece she heard not only her people

but other emergency agencies.

Zealot was razing the entire city. Fires popped up everywhere he flew. Nothing was safe. HR knew Zealot wanted Eddie, but this attack was not something she expected. His focus was usually

better than this. This attack was undefined and erratic.

"He's all over the map. He's not attacking the White House or any of the targets we assumed he

would," Smith said.

"You." HR pointed to an agent.

"Yes, ma'am."

"Go over this data. See if you can find some kind of pattern in this mess."

"On it."

Zealot moving unpredictably around the city was a nightmare for her and her team. Getting the

right response teams to the right place was going to be almost impossible.

"Is he trying to draw out Solomon again?" another agent asked.

"I don't think he needs to try anymore. Eddie knows he needs to stop him. He'll show." After

the way they left things, HR crossed her fingers and prayed that he'd show.

Through all the emergency chatter, one of the Dagger teams broke in. "This is Dagger 9. We're engaging Zealot."

"Dagger 9, what's your position?" HR asked.

"We're at the Washington Monument."

HR turned to the monitors, and the agent controlling the feeds brought up Zealot. While she

watched the situation unfold, a call came in through a secure line. It was the president. "Sorry for the hasty exit. My people thought it best if they got me out as quick as possible." "I understand, sir," HR said.

"My generals have been going over their plans. They intend to engage Zealot. Try not to trip

over each other."

"Don't worry, Mr. President. We'll play nice."

"That's all I can ask." The president hung up.

HR went back to watching Zealot on the screen. Another Dagger team joined Dagger 9, but it didn't seem to slow him down. She heard two fighter jets fly overhead. They came into view on the monitors and launched missiles at him. All four found their target. A bright explosion filled the

screen.

HR wasn't surprised with the military's response. She was taken back a little with the fact that they launched their missiles so close to the monument.

"Dagger 9, status on Zealot?"

There was a moment of silence, then she saw her answer on the screen—Zealot unharmed. There was no sound on the monitors, but she heard Zealot's scream in her earpiece. The teams on the ground fell to their knees and pressed their palms to their ears in pain.

She and her team watched in horror as he turned his fury on the monument and fired his lightning. Almost instantly a red web of cracks became visible. A few of the Dagger agents along with some marines that joined the fight were shooting at Zealot. He continued to fire his lightning as if nothing hit him. The cracks grew wider and glowed with a deeper and more intense shade of red. Things were about to go south, and fast.

"All teams, retreat!" HR said. No sooner had she given the order than the monument exploded. Stone shrapnel flew in every direction, causing untold damage. The only thing left of the obelisk was a small marble stump. A cloud of dust obscured HR's view of the action. One of the screens went blank as a piece of the monument smashed a camera.

"We need more eyes on the situation and more agents on the ground. Call in everyone we can. If we can't stop him here, we won't stop him at all."

Without warning, the command truck shook violently. HR and her team looked around in terror. She reached for the gun cabinet, but she'd never unlock it in time if Zealot decided to attack them. *Who am I kidding? Nothing works against that maniac.* The door of the truck opened, and everyone braced themselves.

In walked Eddie. "Looks like you could use a hand," he said.

HR walked over and punched him in the chest. "Where were you?" A brief smile crossed her lips and then vanished.

"I needed to get my head together. I'm still not all together, but it looks like there are more pressing matters than my mental health." He walked over to the monitors and watched the teams HR had out in the field.

"Zealot showed up out of the blue and started attacking. It looks like he wants to burn down

the entire city," she said.

"Well, I guess this is where we finally get it on. I'm still not sure what counts as a win to the

alien onlookers. A knockout? Death? Do I win if I make him say 'uncle'?"

"I don't know anything about that. All I know is we need you to stop him any way you can. If

that means killing him, so be it."

Eddie nodded and started for the door.

"Wait. We have some things that might help," she added.

"No, thank you," Eddie said. He pointed to his chest. "You can keep your toys. I'll be fine on

my own." He opened the door and flew off.

HR turned back to the monitors and watched Eddie make his way through the city. He stopped and helped a couple trapped in their car—a chunk of monument had hit them, and they couldn't get

out. He stopped again to help someone else.

"Just get Zealot," HR yelled at the screen.

The other agents turned and looked at her.

"He can't help himself," Smith noted. "It's in his nature."

"I know. I just want this over with." She started to pace up and down the small aisle. More Cloak agents materialized around Washington. With the amount of damage Zealot was causing, HR wondered if there would be a city left to rebuild. Another call came in for her. She checked the

phone and had to do a double take.

"This can't be right," she said.

"Who is it?" asked one of the agents.

"It's Agent Jones." HR hit the answer button and put the phone to her ear. "Hello?"

"HR? Hi. It's me. Blair Benson."

HR drew a sigh of relief. The last thing she needed was to find out ghosts were real and calling her from the great beyond. Still, this was a wrinkle she didn't want to deal with now. "I'm kind of busy, Miss Benson. What do you want?"

"I want to help. Eddie should be there by now, and we're on our way."

"Who's 'we'?" A small bit of annoyance crept into her voice.

"Me and Eddie's brother, Lester."

HR knew that if she put her off, she'd keep bothering her and probably get someone hurt or killed. The best thing to do was to bring her in and keep her out of trouble. "Is there a green button on the side of the phone you're using?"

It went quiet for a few seconds. HR heard the phone move around. "Yes, there is."

"I assume you are driving our way now, am I right?"

"Yeah."

"Stop the car. When it comes to a complete stop, hit the button."

"Okay. Will that send out a tracking beacon so you can find us?"

Before HR could answer, the car—along with Lester and Blair—teleported right next to the command truck with a loud thud. She and a few of her agents went out to meet them.

"Wow, that was wild," Blair said as she stepped out of the car.

Lester sat in the driver's seat with a confused and somewhat nauseated look on his face. "Mr. Solomon," Agent Smith said, "would you please get out of the car and follow us?" Lester nodded and got out of the car. He and Blair followed HR and her agents into the truck.

"Take a seat and don't get in the way," HR said.

"But we came to—"

"You came to help. I know. But, as you can see, there's nothing any of us can do. It's all up to Eddie now. The only thing we can do is stay out of their way and help anyone unlucky enough to

get caught in their path."

Lester gave Blair an 'I-told-you-so' look and started playing with his phone. Blair fidgeted in her chair. "I don't want to just sit here and look at a wall of screens."

"Unfortunately, for you, that's all you'll be doing," HR retorted.

Blair grumbled, leaned back, and closed her eyes.

CHAPTER TWENTY-SEVEN

Lester sat in his chair and stared at his phone. He was playing chess with the game's AI. Normally he'd challenge one of several live opponents he found over the years, but the Wi-Fi was cut off, so he made do with the computer. Every now and then, he glanced up to see what Blair was doing or to look at the bank of screens and watch the action outside. But he really couldn't care less.

As long as his corner of the world was left alone, he'd be fine.

"I want to get out of here," Blair whispered to Lester.

He put his phone down and leaned in toward her. "Are you crazy? Look at it out there. It's a literal war zone." Lester couldn't believe her. He'd never understand her desire to jump into dangerous situations like the one going on. If he had his way, they'd still be in Philadelphia. He still

cared for Blair and didn't want to see her do anything reckless with her life.

Unfortunately, revealing his true feelings for Eddie pushed her away for good. *One more thing he's taken from me*, he thought to himself. Any chance of reconciliation was long gone. He didn't know how or when, but he would find a way to hurt Eddie and make him understand his pain.

"There are people out there that need help," she continued. "If I can offer that to at least one

person, then I'll be happy."

Lester sat back and shook his head. The whole world had gone crazy, and he seemed to be the only sane one left. Running into a city on fire was just plain stupid, but no one was going to listen to him.

"Fine. You want to go out there and play hero, be my guest." He pointed to the door at the far

side of the aisle. "But they're not going to let you go, so you might as well accept it and wait."

She sat back and folded her arms in anger.

Lester loved her passion. It was one of the first things he noticed about her when she started working for him. Occasionally, a case would cross his desk that looked unwinnable. Blair would see it and convince him to take it on. And more times than not, he'd win the case. Now her passion was

going to get her hurt, or worse.

An explosion rocked the command truck, and the agents scrambled to find the cause. The power in the truck flickered, then went out. Emergency lights came on, but they weren't very bright.

They gave off just enough light to keep people from bumping into each other.

Blair looked around and stood up. "This is our chance," she said. "Let's go." She grabbed for

Lester, but he swatted her hand away.

"Sit down. Who knows what's happening out there."

"I'm going," she said.

While HR and her team worked on getting the power back, Blair ran for the door. HR swung

her head around just in time to see Blair slip out. She turned toward Lester.

He raised his hands in surrender. "I told her not to do it."

HR flashed him a not so nice look. "Seriously?" She turned to her agents. "Agent Smith, get that power back on. Then reestablish communication with the Cloak agents and find out what their

situation are."

"What are you going to do?" he asked.

"Mr. Solomon and I are going after his girlfriend before something happens to her."

Lester stood up and backed up. "I'm not going anywhere," he said. He put his hands up to signal his desire to be left out of this. "She's an adult. She can do her own thing—even if that thing

is stupid."

"I'm making it your thing." HR grabbed him by the arm and pulled him out of the corner. For a woman on the short side, she had quite a bit of strength to her. He tried to resist, but it was no use. "When we find her, I'm sending both of you back to the Cloak-Dagger facility where you'll be

under armed guard until this situation is over. I've had enough of you two."

"Me? I didn't even want to be here in the first place," he said. "I tried to talk her out of this

ridiculous idea. All the way from Philly, I did what I could to get her to see reason."

"Well, you had your chance. It's my turn now, and that means putting you two somewhere safe and out of the way." HR opened a cabinet by the door and pulled out two guns. "This is no ordinary gun. It's a laser pistol, so be careful or you'll blow your leg off." She slid her gun into her holster and

handed the other to Lester.

"I don't do guns," he said and pushed it away.

HR slammed it against his chest and held it there. "I don't think you should have one either, but it isn't safe out there. So you will take this gun, and you will help me find Miss. Benson. Do you understand?"

Lester took the gun and nodded. "Whatever you say, boss."

"Good. The sooner we find her, the sooner I can get back and deal with this." She walked over to the door and held it open for him.

Lester sighed and shuffled his feet as he walked past her.

He hated being out in this. Between the fires lighting up the city with an orange hue and the black clouds of smoke drifting around, he felt like he was in a disaster movie. But this wasn't going to be settled in two hours.

He thought about how this whole situation would affect him. He'd need a new secretary. Find movers to put Blair's furniture back in her apartment. And then there's Eddie. If he beat Zealot, Lester wouldn't hear the end of it—all about how he did it, how wonderful he was, people would love him. But if he lost, people would be sad for a while, but at least he'd be free from his brother's shadow once and for all. That last thought made being out in the inferno a little more bearable.

From up ahead, HR yelled for him. "Keep up!" The smoke made it tough to see, and sirens went off everywhere, making it hard to hear. He quickened his pace and caught up with HR.

"Do you have a plan or are we going to run around hoping to run into her?" Lester asked.

"She couldn't have gotten far. We'll find her soon enough." HR took off down the street and waved for Lester to follow.

In the distance, he heard another explosion and wondered if it was from the fires or from Eddie and Zealot fighting. Either way he didn't want to be out any longer than he had to be. He caught up to and passed HR.

"Blair," he called out, "where are you?"

He saw something up ahead. There was too much smoke to make out what it was, but he thought it was as good a direction to try. As luck would have it, it was Blair. She was helping a woman and her daughter. There was a car off the road and up on the sidewalk, smashed against a

pole. Blair lifted the little girl out of the car while her mother ran around to them.

"Looks like you were right. She didn't get too far, after all," he said, relieved. Not so much because they found Blair but because this was about to be over and he could get to somewhere less

dangerous.

"Miss Benson, you need to come with me," HR said. Lester stayed back as she went over to see what Blair was doing. HR said something to the woman he couldn't hear and pointed back the way

they came. The woman and her daughter ran past him.

He walked over to Blair and HR. "Can we go now? I'd like to get out of this hellscape, please." Lester started walking back toward the command truck. Part of a building suddenly collapsed, and

he jumped back. The way was blocked. He ran back to the two women. "Now what?"

A loud screeching noise erupted from behind them. Zealot flew by. He was using his bansheelike scream to cause the buildings in the area to crumble.

"Run!" HR yelled.

The three of them ran deeper into the city. They found a store with the front wall mostly gone

and ducked inside.

"Do you think he saw us?" Blair asked.

"If he did, we'd be dead by now," Lester said. There were some folding chairs scattered on the

floor. He opened one up and sat down. "I need a break."

"Smith, this is HR. What's the situation?" HR's communicator crackled with static. It sounded like someone was trying to answer, but it was garbled. "Say again," she said. This time the static

cleared enough to hear him.

"Zealot is circling our area. It looks like he might make a run at the White House," Smith said.

"Can we get any of our people over there?"

"We're moving some to our location now. I'm not sure if it will do any good," Smith said. The

connection went dead, and HR slid the communicator into her pocket.

"Well, we can't go back now. Too much heat." HR opened another of the folding chairs and sat down. "We'll have to hunker down here for the time being. Hopefully, Zealot won't be back this

way, and we can figure out our next move."

"I thought our next move was dropping Blair and myself in a secure location under guard. What happened to that?" Lester said. His self-preservation was in high gear. He wanted to be anywhere

but here.

"We're using our troop teleporters to move our people around the city. We're going to have to

wait to move you two."

"Well, that's just great." Lester threw his hands up and brought them down, smacking his legs.

Blair grabbed a chair.

The three of them sat and looked out at what used to be the front window. From their left, a car went sailing by. The fight had found its way to them. They jumped up as Zealot picked up

another car and threw it past the store front. Eddie blasted it with a blue beam from his hands.

While HR and Blair watched the fight, Lester caressed the gun in his hand. *I'd love to take a shot at Eddie and end this fight.* He got up and moved around to the far right of the store front where some shelves blocked the women's view of him. He raised the gun and aimed it at Eddie. He took a deep breath and pulled the trigger. A flash of light shot out of the gun and passed in front of Eddie,

barely missing him.

HR and Blair ran over, and Lester dropped the gun.

"What are you doing? Did you...?" Blair asked.

"I, uh..." he began. "No, I—"

Before he could say anything further, HR cuffed him—at least they looked like handcuffs but with a purple glow to them. "This will keep you from doing anything else stupid," she said. Lester tried to move away from her, but he couldn't. "Nice try, but these cuffs will keep you with me at all

times. Wherever I go, you go."

"This is illegal," Lester said. "You can't do this to me."

"You just tried to shoot your brother with an energy weapon. I can do a lot worse to you, but I

won't. Not now."

Blair shook her head and walked away from the two of them.

Lester's need to help finish the fight blew up in his face. Worse, Zealot headed straight for them.

"Guys, I think we have—"

Before Zealot reached them, Eddie intercepted him. The two flew off out of their line of sight.

HR ran out onto the street, and Lester couldn't help but follow. The communicator rang, and she answered it. "Go ahead."

"Ma'am, Eddie and Zealot have moved out of the city. It looks like they're out at Rock Creek

Park," Smith said.

"We need to get out there. Can we teleport?"

"No, but we've sent a self-driving vehicle your way."

A few minutes later an armored Humvee pulled up to the three of them, and they all piled in.

HR turned around to Lester and Blair. "No matter what happens you stay in this truck. Do you

understand me?"

"I thought I had to follow you everywhere." Lester sounded like a child talking back to his

mom. Blair hit him in the arm. "Ow!" The purple glow disappeared.

"You're still going to be restrained, but now you won't have to leave the safety of the truck. Better?" HR said.

"We're still going to be close to the fighting. I won't feel better until it's done, and I can get

back to my life," he said.

"If we let you get back to your life..." HR said. "What you did back there was beyond stupid,

and we'll see you pay for it."

"Good luck," Lester said.

The Humvee made its way through the city, avoiding cars and downed buildings. As they got

closer to the park, they saw red and blue flashes of light and heard sounds of thunder.

Lester hoped the end was near.

CHAPTER TWENTY-EIGHT

Before Eddie confronted Zealot, he wanted to help whoever he could and clear a path for evacuations. Many people made their way out of the city by foot or on bikes. The number of fires and collapsed buildings made evacuation by car almost impossible. Only four-wheel drive vehicles were able to get through areas with smaller amounts of debris. He watched some trucks that looked like HR's unit make their way through the mess as well.

After rescuing a couple from a second-floor apartment, he used his energy blasts to clear rubble from the road. He heard an explosion behind him and turned to see Zealot blasting cars left on the street.

"I guess this is where I come in," he said.

As he made his way to intercept Zealot, he saw HR, Lester, and Blair duck into a bombed-out store. *They might need my help.* As he made his way over, a car flew past him. He looked up and found Zealot staring at him. Red sparks shot from his eyes and hands. The gem in his chest pulsated like a strobe light.

Out of nowhere, a laser bolt flew by, barely missing Eddie. It looked like it came from the

direction of the store. "Hey, watch it," he yelled.

Then he noticed Zealot moving toward the trio in the store. With a quickness even he didn't know he had, Eddie flew in with a shoulder block and knocked him backward. He charged up his fist with his energy and punched Zealot square in the jaw, launching him into the air. He flew up after him and blasted him in the chest. The intensity of the force sent Zealot flying out of the city

limits.

Eddie chased him down to a park with walking trails. There was a path of downed trees carved out where Zealot crashed.

Eddie landed and picked up a sign that had been knocked over and mangled. "Rock Creek Park." He tossed the sign to the side and walked in the direction of Zealot's crash site. "I always

wanted to come here. Hopefully, I'll get the chance under better circumstances."

He didn't have to look too hard to find his opponent. Red lightning and Zealot's scream let him know exactly where he was. Eddie followed the noise of Zealot's rampaging deeper into the woods. When he found him, Zealot was darting back and forth like a wild animal. The time he fought him

in Kansas City, he seemed much more in control. Now he was plain mad.

Eddie pep talked himself. "Okay, energy blast and then charge in. I got this."

He leveled his hands in Zealot's direction. But before he could charge up, Zealot turned and ran straight for him. He closed the distance faster than expected and knocked Eddie backward. A tree burst into splinters, and Eddie smashed into the ground. He shook his head and stood up. A small

crater was left behind.

"I felt that." Eddie rubbed the back of his head.

Zealot circled him, growling, and swung his clawed hand at him.

"Something's definitely off with you, I hope I don't have to worry about that."

Zealot just kept circling. He stopped and let out a scream that knocked Eddie off his feet, and

Zealot pounced on him then.

Eddie put his arms up to keep from being ripped apart. While he had found out he was bullet proof, Zealot's claws were something quite different. They ripped through his shirt and skin, digging into his forearms. He rolled and hit Zealot with an elbow, then got back to his feet. His arms dripped with blood. The blood itself was a shock—seeing that it was blue was an even bigger one.

"Great time to find this out."

Zealot charged him again, but Eddie side stepped and punched him in the back of the head.

Zealot stumbled but was quick to regain his balance and spun back around. Eddie planted his feet, ready for another charge, but Zealot jumped over him and hit him with red lightning. His body

seized up, and he dropped to his knees as Zealot rained more lightning on him from behind.

Eddie was thrown forward, and his face drove into the ground. Zealot jumped on his back and continued to maul him. The pain to his back was excruciating. He shoved hard off the ground, and Zealot jumped into the air.

He hovered there, staring at Eddie, then launched himself skywards. Eddie followed him. When

he cleared the trees, Zealot surprised him from behind with his own move and started to squeeze.

Eddie got the wind knocked out of him and couldn't catch his breath. He struggled to free himself. Zealot squeezed tighter, and the gem in his chest dug into his back—he could feel it cutting

into him, the heat burning him.

The lack of oxygen made Eddie lightheaded. His vision blurred and all went dark.

* * *

Eddie woke up as he crashed through the trees and tumbled onto one of the walking paths. He gulped for air. Never in all his life had he experienced a fight like this one. He stood up shakily when Zealot flew in and drove his fists into his torso. Eddie tumbled backward down over an embankment and onto a huge outcropping of rocks. He bounced off the rocks and landed on the forest floor.

Zealot walked toward him. "Deathhhhh for you," he said. He grabbed him by what was left of his shirt and threw him into another tree.

Eddie's head slammed against the trunk, and his teeth rattled. The situation started to worry him. If he lost this battle, no one would be safe from Zealot. His anxiety flared up. Blood dripped over his eyes. His heart raced, breathing quickened. *This is not the time.* If only his meds worked for him. He looked around as if he just realized where he was. All he wanted to do right now was run away and find someplace to hide.

Zealot propelled himself forward and threw a punch that knocked Eddie through another tree.

He fired his lightning at him, and the surrounding area burst into flames.

Eddie laid on the ground. He didn't want to get back up, but knew he had to. He never endured this level of pain before. Another round of lightning hit, and he was thrown back like a rag doll. He landed on his back with his legs folded over him. He went limp and rolled to his side.

"Deathhh. Deathhhh to you, championnn," Zealot hissed.

Eddie reached up and dug his nails into a tree to pull himself up. Even that hurt. As he let go, blood trickled from his hands. His entire body screamed in pain. He felt his face swell up. His arms and back stung from the claw marks, like his skin was on fire. He wiped dirt from his eyes and tried to focus on Zealot who was creeping toward him. Eddie took up a defensive stance, but he got

lightheaded again and fell to one knee.

Zealot stopped and laughed. At least that's what it seemed like to Eddie. The sound was shrill and felt like shards of glass being dragged across his brain. Eddie leapt into the air, hoping to fly away and regroup, but the sound messed with his equilibrium so much that he shot off sideways. He bounced off some trees and fell back toward the earth. Zealot laughed harder. Eddie raised his hand

and shot a bolt of energy, but it was so far off that Zealot didn't even flinch.

"I win," he said. He took his time walking over to Eddie. His hands crackled and sparked with

red lightning. His smile, if you could call it that, went from ear to ear while he bared his fanged teeth.

A gun shot rang out and hit Zealot in the back. He turned around and a police officer knelt in

the distance.

"You two, stop and keep your hands where I can see them," the officer yelled out. Eddie put his hands up. "Officer, wait, I'm the good guy. You want to point that—"

But it was too late.

Zealot extended his arms to either side and blasted lightening at both Eddie and the officer. The officer was dead before he hit the ground, and Eddie flew back another few feet. Zealot turned

toward him. "Time's up," he said. But then something caught his attention.

Headlights bounced up and down through the trees. The lights went dark, and Eddie heard people talking. He focused all his energy and listened. His eyes widened—it was Lester and the others. He struggled to get his footing back. It looked like Zealot was talking to someone, but no one else was there. He grunted, then waved at something. Eddie didn't know what to make of this. Zealot turned his attention to Eddie and flashed a grin before launching himself in his friends' direction. This was his nightmare—not being able to defend the ones he loved. He fell back and

closed his eyes.

"Are you going to lie there, or are you going to help them?" a familiar voice asked.

Eddie fought to open his eyes. His wife stood in front of him. "What? I must be dead." He

gathered his strength and sat himself up. "Did I die?"

"No, Eddie, you're very much alive." She smiled at him.

He broke down in tears. "You're dead because I couldn't save you. Now everyone else I care

about is going to die too."

"Then you need to get up and do something about it." She nodded toward the lights and noise.

"They can't bring him down. Only you can."

"Do you see me? I can barely stand, let alone fight. I'm the wrong guy for this, and now

everyone is going to pay." Eddie fell back down and put his hands over his head.

"This is not the man I married," she said. "The Eddie Solomon I knew would never let

anything get in the way of defending the people who needed him."

"I lost you," he said, sobbing. "I lost you, and nothing mattered anymore."

"I love you, Eddie, and as much as I want you to be with me again, I need you to get up and

fight back. You are their only hope."

"But what about us? I'm sorry for... Emma, I..."

She leaned down and put a finger on his lips. "We'll be together, later. Right now, you need to

get up and fight." She backed up and started to fade away.

"No! Wait!"

"Get up and fight, Eddie! Get up and fight!" she yelled. Then she disappeared completely.

CHAPTER TWENTY-NINE

HR looked in the rear-view mirror and watched Blair and Lester bounce around in their seats. The ride wasn't the smoothest. HR drove on sidewalks, over debris, and through forest. She wished just one of her team members stayed with her to help, but they were all dealing with the aftermath of Zealot's rampage. She was stuck with these two. Blair, who wanted to do the right thing but had zero training. And Lester. Someone so filled with hate for his brother, he'd rather side with the

enemy. This wouldn't be easy.

"Must you hit every bump you see?" Lester cried.

HR felt him hit the back of her seat as they motored through the forest. Knowing he was being inconvenienced gave her a small bit of joy. His cuffs glowed purple again, likely from all the bumps. She smiled a little more inside. Up ahead a clearing came into view. She pulled off the road and cut

the engine.

"Looks like something came down hard here." She jumped out to examine the scene.

A loud thud came from the truck. Lester groaned.

"If I had to guess, someone crashed here. Hard to say if it was Eddie or Zealot," HR said. She

walked around the area slowly and picked up broken pieces of tree, inspecting them.

Blair ran around to Lester's door. His face was pressed against the window. She opened the

door, and he fell out and slid to within a few feet of HR.

"You better get up before you get full of splinters," HR said.

Lester mumbled something under his breath.

"Do you think they're near?" Blair asked.

"Oh yes, I can't wait to get in the middle of those two," Lester said as he brushed himself off.

Off in the distance, they heard thunder and more crashing trees. HR turned toward the noise and started walking. Lester was compelled to follow. Blair ran to catch up. The group didn't say much as they made their way deeper into the park. Lester grumbled as he tried to slow down, but his feet slid through debris. He stumbled forward, then picked up his pace. HR scanned the forest with

her flashlight, looking for the best path to take. She had the laser gun in her other hand.

"Do you have an extra gun for me?" Blair asked.

"No, I only have this one." HR did have a smaller one in a holster clipped to the back of her belt, but no way she'd give either of them another weapon after the stunt Lester pulled. HR's mind swirled with all kinds of contingencies. Plans to deal with Zealot if he won. Plans for Eddie if he won. She couldn't wait to let Lester in on the plans she had for him. She was going to relish

throwing him in a deep, dark hole where no one would ever find him.

The sound of trees splintering came closer. The ground shook under their feet. HR had a horrible feeling in her gut. A blue bolt of energy shot out of the dark and passed by the group. HR dove for cover, pulling Lester down with her. Blair screamed and ducked behind a tree. More

thunder could be heard not too far from where they were.

"We're close. We'll need to be careful," HR said as she stood up and dusted dirt from her pants.

Lester went to check on Blair, but the bond with HR kept him just out of reach. "How long do

I need to wear these things?" he asked.

HR could tell he was getting more frustrated with every passing minute. She had no sympathy for him. "You'll keep them on until I say otherwise. Let's go." She paused. "Wait, I smell smoke." In

the distance, there was a burning glow among the trees. "Great, that's all we need."

"Maybe we should go back. I don't want to walk into a forest fire," Lester said.

"We'll be all right. We just need to be extra careful." HR continued toward the fire, and Lester reluctantly followed. Blair ran up to stay next to HR. Gray smoke filtered through the trees and the glow of the fire intensified. HR felt Lester trying to pull away from her. She turned a small knob on

her belt and drew him closer.

"Really," Lester shouted.

HR stopped to scold him, but something caught her attention. "Do you hear that?" She cocked her head and listened. The noise grew louder, faster. It sounded like an oncoming train. She looked

around for cover and hid behind the biggest tree she could find. The others followed her lead.

"Do you see anything?" Blair asked.

HR peeked out. "Oh no." Her voice dripped with dread as she moved back behind the tree. She

grabbed her spare gun and tossed it to Blair. "Zealot's coming. Get ready."

"What?" Blair screeched. She fumbled with the gun. "I thought you said you only had one

weapon?"

"Now's not the time. Just get ready to shoot."

"No gun for me?" Lester asked.

HR slapped him and pointed in Zealot's direction. "You're lucky I'm not throwing you at him."

She turned and planted her feet, ready to take on Zealot.

Blair held the gun out in front of her. Her legs trembled.

Zealot was almost on top of them when another similar noise came in from their right. Eddie— with a bright blue glow none of them had seen before—flew in and grabbed Zealot in a bear hug,

then drove him up into the air.

HR jumped out from behind the tree and pointed her gun in the air after them. Between the

smoke and the trees, she quickly lost sight of the two.

"We need to find them. We need to get back to the truck. I'll call command and see if they can

track them."

"Great. Let's go," Lester said. His feet moved, but he didn't get anywhere. He sighed and

turned to face HR in disgust.

"Nothing's changed. I'm not letting you go. You'll stay tethered to me until this is over and I

can get you back to headquarters."

"This is illegal," Lester shouted. "I have rights, and you and your 'organization' are denying me

those rights."

"You tried to kill your brother," HR said. She grabbed him by his shirt and shook him as she talked. "And in turn knowingly offered aid to an enemy alien. That's reason enough to throw you in

a cell and forget you're there." She let him go, and he dropped to the ground. "Now let's go."

HR's pace was just shy of running. Blair lagged behind. Lester fell and got dragged the rest of the way to the truck. His clothes were torn up, and he bled from cuts up and down his body. HR picked him up and shoved him into the truck. Blair crawled into the back, breathing heavily.

"How's it feel to be controlled?" Blair asked. Her face showed only disdain for him.

HR dialed her phone. "Smith, this is HR. What's your situation?"

"We have almost everything under control. Our teams are assisting local emergency agencies with the mess. Fires still rage, but they are contained."

"That's good news. Were you able to keep tabs on Eddie and Zealot?"

"We have a lock on them now. Do you need their coordinates?"

"Yes. If we have any free people, send them to me. There's a fire here that needs to be extinguished." HR tapped the screen on the dashboard, sending her information to the command truck. Eddie's location popped up on the screen with a red line leading from their spot to his.

"Is that everything?" Smith asked.

"That will be all." HR hung up and put the truck in gear. The blip on the screen wasn't that far from them, but their altitude was at 60,000 feet and climbing. A green circle showed an estimated landing area. She pointed to it and said, "That's where we're going. When this is over, I hope Eddie comes out on top, or the planet is screwed."

HR hit the gas and took off through the trees. She wasn't a religious person, but she said a silent prayer. If there was a god, she hoped he'd let things go in her favor.

CHAPTER THIRTY

E ddie clambered to his feet. Zealot had a huge head start on him. He couldn't fail his friends—

he needed to do better. He ran and jumped into the air but fell back.

"No, not now," he said. He ran faster and tried again, but he got the same result. *What's happening to me?* His injuries shouldn't keep him from using his powers. He made a fist and shot a

bolt of energy through the trees. *Okay, that works.*

He closed his eyes and cleared his mind. His wife was right. He still doubted himself. He'd been feeling better about his life, but deep down he still felt like he failed Emma and that he'd end up

failing everyone else.

"I'm not that guy anymore," he said. "I'm not going to let anxiety and depression control me. Not when the people I love need me the most." He clenched his fists and focused all his energy into

one single thought. *Stop Zealot.*

He felt a tingling sensation and a surge of power. He opened his eyes. He was glowing, and a bright blue aura surrounded him. A grin crept onto his face, and he propelled himself into the air. He felt faster and stronger than before. He didn't know if this was a natural progression of his powers, or if he tapped into a reserve. All he cared about now was catching Zealot and finally

putting an end to him.

He pushed himself forward faster and caught up to Zealot who was charging up in mid-flight. His friends were just a few yards away. Eddie wrapped his arms around Zealot and squeezed as hard as he could. There was a popping sound, and Zealot gave out a howl of pain. He adjusted his flight path and carried them both straight up into the sky.

When they cleared the trees, Eddie let him go and punched him in the chest, which sent him higher into the air. Some of Zealot's red tubing came loose, and red sparks flew from the ends.

Eddie shot off another round of energy bolts and sent Zealot even higher.

Eddie's life—since the fire—replayed over and over in his mind. The good times he had coming back home. The dark thoughts of suicide. The second chance he never asked for but was blessed with, even if it came at a cost. He wasn't going to let anything, or anyone, get in his way

again. His anxiety had consumed him so completely he thought he'd never see daylight again.

Yet here he was. Not only living but doing what he always wanted to do—help people who

couldn't help themselves. This time, though, it was the entire planet.

He wouldn't give Zealot the chance to win.

Eddie charged again. He focused all his energy into his hand and punched Zealot in his jaw and felt it pop. Zealot spun backward a few times, and Eddie caught one of his ankles. He swung him around and threw him back to Earth.

Eddie hadn't noticed how high he'd taken Zealot until he turned around. The air was cold, and he noticed ice crystals were forming on his skin. He was probably higher than he reached with the alien exo-suit.

Zealot plummeted with his back to the ground. He shot off his lightning, but Eddie dodged the bolts. He opened his jaw to banshee-scream, but Eddie launched a punch to his throat and sped his descent. Zealot grabbed at his neck, coughing and choking. A look of determination came over him,

then he righted himself and flew after Eddie. He charged and let loose a storm of red lightning.

The light and electricity almost blinded Eddie, as if a flash bang went off. Then he felt a strike to the head. Eddie spun around a few times when Zealot hit him again. They struggled in the air and exchanged punches until Eddie somehow wrapped his legs around Zealot's chest. He began driving his fists into his face over and over. He squeezed his legs tighter while Zealot tried to slash at him.

Blood splattered into the air, but Eddie didn't let go. He propelled them both toward Earth as fast

as he could.

Zealot weakened with every punch to the face, and the fight in him eventually left. He started to go limp as Eddie pummeled him. He was bloody and broken. The left side of his face was caved in and the skin—if you could call it that—split so bad across the top of his head, you could see his

skull.

"You wanted this," Eddie screamed. "You wanted this fight, so here you go. You got it!" Eddie saw the ground coming up fast and didn't care. If dying meant that Zealot would die too, he was

okay with that.

He unwrapped his legs and stomped at his enemy's chest, pushing him down, all while he

continued to punch him in the head. The force and speed were so much that it caused a sonic boom.

Eddie let out a yell as he and Zealot hit the ground.

* * *

HR slammed on the breaks and jumped out of the Humvee. Lester came tumbling out behind

her. The GPS beeped, and everyone looked up.

"Looks like we're in the right spot," Blair said. She pointed over to Eddie and Zealot fighting— mere dots in the sky.

"Is it my imagination or do they look like they're falling fast?" Lester said.

HR strained her neck to see. Red lightning flashed in the sky, but she didn't see much else.

"They're still too far up."

"We should back up," Blair said.

"We don't know where they're going to come down," HR said. "We'll stay here until we can get

a better idea of the situation."

HR leaned in and grabbed the pair of binoculars from the center console. They were confiscated from an alien that came to observe Earth's vulnerabilities to invasion. Cloak agents got wind of it, and HR sent in a Dagger unit to subdue the alien. It was eventually released and given a warning to take back to their kind: Earth was protected, and an invasion ill-conceived. No sign of it

or its kind had been reported since.

HR turned a dial on the side and magnified her view. "It looks like he's riding Zealot back to

Earth," she said.

"Leave it to my brother to showboat. Even when the world is at stake," Lester said with a large

helping of sarcasm.

"Shut up, Lester," Blair said and punched him in the gut. "I'm tired of your crap."

He doubled over in a heap.

"Well done, Miss Benson!" HR said proudly. Blair was a nuisance, but seeing her stand up to

Lester impressed her.

Suddenly, they heard a booming noise. Eddie and Zealot descended at wicked speed.

"Get behind the truck," HR yelled.

They scrambled to the other side of the Humvee just as Eddie and Zealot hit the ground. The explosion their impact created was like a nuclear bomb. The trucked lifted off the ground. HR and Lester sailed into a tree. Lester slammed against her. Blair soared past them and landed in a shallow

creek. Dust and debris rained down, and everyone's ears rang.

HR got to her feet and steadied herself. She thought she might have a concussion as she felt

dizzy and sick.

Lester stood up and fell right back down. "I don't feel so good," he said in a weak, raspy voice.

"I don't care how you feel. Get up," HR said.

Blair limped over, all wet from the creek. From the extent of the debris, HR figured the blast must have had a radius of about three hundred feet. The truck was on its side wedged between two

trees.

"Do you hear that?" HR asked.

"Yeah, it's coming from the crater," Blair said.

The three of them made their way over to ground zero. The crater was about seven feet deep and twenty feet wide. The fact that anything within its radius survived was a miracle. They moved closer to the edge. Eddie and Zealot still grappled, but neither of them looked like they had much

strength left.

Zealot raised his head to the trio. He stepped toward them, but before he could do anything else, Eddie punched a hole straight through his chest. Zealot's gem flew across the crater and

shattered. He looked down at the gaping wound and fell to his knees, then onto his face.

Eddie smiled at his friends. He gave them a thumbs up, then fell backward in the dirt.

HR and Blair slid down the crater and ran over to Eddie. HR glanced back and saw Lester still at the edge of the crater. The control over his cuffs must have been damaged when they hit the tree.

"Lester, don't wander off."

"Wouldn't think of it," Lester said as he dug around in the dirt.

HR tried not to let Lester distract her. She needed to focus on Eddie. The damage he sustained would have killed any normal man. The gashes in his arms ran deep. Burns littered his chest and legs. She guessed he might even have a few broken bones. HR turned to check on Lester again. He still stood there, kicking dirt and rocks. Eddie started to cough up blood. And there was a pool of blood under him. He needed medical treatment now. HR pulled off her jacket, rolled it up, and placed it under his head.

HR put her fingers against Eddie's neck and wrist to see if she could feel a pulse. She did, but it was weak. She ripped a sleeve off her shirt and pressed it against one of the deeper wounds on his chest.

"Blair, find my phone! We need help if Eddie has any chance of surviving."

Blair nodded and ran up the side of the crater. A few minutes later, she returned with the phone. The screen was badly broken. HR turned it on hoping it would still work. After what felt like hours, the phone came to life. She ran her finger against the broken glass to initiate the call.

"Agent Smith, this is HR. Can you hear me?"

"We read you, ma'am. We've been tracking you but lost your signal. We heard an explosion and thought the worst."

"I need a medical crew at my position asap! I don't care where you have to pull them from. This is priority."

"Right away, ma'am." The connection went silent.

Green teleportation doors opened and the Cloak-Dagger med crew appeared.

"You're going to be all right, Eddie," Blair said. "Just hang on."

Two medics rushed over with a stretcher and loaded him on and back through the teleportation door.

HR grabbed Blair's wrist. "Where's Lester?"

Blair looked around and shrugged her shoulders. "I don't know. Last I remember he was with

us at the edge of the crater."

HR needed to find him, but taking care of everyone's injuries were first on her list. She and

Blair followed the medics through, and the portal snapped shut behind them.

* * *

High overhead, Eoch forces attacked the Thiar armada, destroying them ship by ship. As Earth's citizens stared upwards, the sky burst into brilliant colors. Unbeknownst to them, the life of every person on the planet was about to change, forever.

CHAPTER THIRTY-ONE

E ight months later.

Eddie opened his eyes and quickly shut them again. The light was too bright. He had a headache, and his mouth was dry. He slowly opened his eyes again. There were I.V. tubes in his arms. *Where am I?* He tried to remember what happened. Everything in his head was fuzzy. He remembered his childhood, his wife, coming home to Philadelphia. But after that, he wasn't sure. He sat up and scanned the room. It looked like a hospital room, but it seemed more military than civilian—concrete walls and a large mirror on the far wall. The sound of machines beeping drifted into his consciousness.

A nurse rushed in. "Well, look who's sitting up." She checked the instruments and jotted down the information on a tablet. She smiled and took a hold of Eddie's hand. "There are a lot of people who are going to want to see you." She ran back out of the room.

There was a television in the corner of the room. The remote sat on the table to his right. He tried to grab it, but the tubes and his sore arm kept him back. He reached again, and one of the I.V. tubes came loose. An alarm went off on a machine.

The door opened, and a doctor walked in, followed by two women. *Blair.* He smiled. But the

other one. He tried to think.

"What's going on in here?" the doctor asked. He fumbled with the tubes. "It's been a while since you were awake. You're going to need a lot of physical therapy if you expect to regain your

mobility."

"Therapy? How long have I been out?" Eddie looked around confused.

"Eddie," Blair said as she walked over and sat on the edge of his bed, "you've been in a coma for eight months."

"Coma?"

"After your fight with Zealot, you collapsed. We brought you here. The doctors were able to stabilize you and found a way to get through your rhino hide to get those tubes in." Blair took his

hand in hers and smiled. "We were afraid you'd never wake up."

"I knew you would," the smaller-statured woman said. She patted him on the leg. "You're too

much of a pain in the neck to stay asleep."

"Yes, that's right. HR." He chuckled. "And Zealot—I remember killing Zealot. It's everything

after that's hazy."

"I'm surprised you remember anything after the beating you took," the doctor said.

"But you're awake, and now we can work on getting you back to normal," Blair said.

"Get your rest. Tomorrow we start therapy." The doctor left the room.

HR patted him on the leg again and followed the doctor out.

Blair stayed behind. She pulled a chair over next to his bed and sat down. "I guess you have

some questions."

"What happened to Zealot?"

"Some Dagger agents brought his body back to examine," she said.

"What about the Eoch and the Thiar? Do we know what happened to them?"

Blair looked away and then back. "That's a bit of a long story."

"And where's Lester? I figured he'd be here."

"Well, when we were in that burnt-out store..."

"I remember that. Zealot had you guys pinned down. Someone tried to shoot him but almost
hit me."

Blair looked away again. Her face flushed red. *Is that embarrassment?*

"If it was you, I'm not mad. You just need some work on your aim." Eddie smiled to reassure
her.

"No, it wasn't me. Eddie..." She adjusted herself in her chair and looked him in the eyes.

"...Lester tried to shoot you."

"What?" he exclaimed. "We've had our differences, but he would never try and kill me."

"Lester slid into a very dark place. Whatever bitterness he had for you grew into full blown
hate."

"But where is he? I want to see him."

"We don't know. He disappeared after the fight. No one's seen or heard from him since that
day."

"And what about the aliens? I won, so I guess that means the Eoch won."

"They did. And we're dealing with the fallout of that too. And I do mean fallout."

Eddie arched his eyebrows. "What do you mean?"

"When the Eoch destroyed the Thiar, they did it while in orbit. Their fleet of ships were massive. Pieces of spaceship fell to Earth for days. Not to mention the cloud of radiation that

hovered in the sky for weeks."

"Radiation? Is it okay to go outside?"

"Yeah, there was no damage to the planet. The people. That's a different story."

"Meaning?"

"Let's just say you're not the only one with superpowers anymore."

"Really?"

"Not everyone. As far as we can figure, there have been only a few hundred people affected."

"I guess that's not too bad."

"It can be. If half of those people use their powers for selfish gain and the police can't stop

them. Well, you know how it goes."

Eddie cocked his head and noticed she wore a Cloak-Dagger uniform. He reached out and

touched her arm. "And then this happened," he said.

Blair's face reddened again. "HR brought me in as a liaison between the organization and the press. I'm actually pretty good at it." She sat up a little straighter and puffed her chest out. "I don't

want to brag, but I've met the president."

"Wow. Get a load of you." Eddie felt a swell of pride come over him. Blair wasn't blood, but the time he spent with her over the last few years, in his mind, made her family. And seeing as how Lester vanished, she was the last family he had. "Do you think we could watch some TV? Maybe it

can help me get caught up on everything that's happened."

"I think I can do that." Blair grabbed the remote and gave it to Eddie.

He scrolled through the guide and stopped on a news channel. "This should be a good start." The reporter was talking about the rise in powered people and how the president and his handpicked team planned to enact new laws to protect both them and non-powered people. "Just

what we need. More laws."

"It'll be fine. HR is on the team. She won't let anyone get too out of hand."

"Well, I hope so."

Eddie turned it to another news channel. This one looked like a rally gone wrong with two sides fighting and yelling across barricades. Police were on both sides. They pushed back the mobs to

keep them away from each other.

A reporter stood in front of the barricades, microphone in his hand. "The 'March for Human Rights'—which started as a peaceful protest against the increasing number of powered—has turned violent. Another group, representing the superpowered, had intersected with the march and tempers ran over. Police were called in to separate the two sides. Neither side will back down from their

stances, and crowds on both sides are growing."

Eddie muted the TV. "Great. How long before my name gets dragged into this mess?"

"It already has. HR provided as much political cover as she could, and the president said without you the world would be lost. But there are some groups that blame you for the rise of

superpowered people."

"Oh that's just swell." Eddie fell back against his pillow.

"Don't worry about it. They're in the minority. As far as the general public is concerned, you

are a hero." Blair's attention turned to the protest on the television. "Eddie, turn up the TV."

He looked over at the screen and saw that the two sides were now scattered. He turned the volume up. People were screaming and running for their lives. Red bolts of energy flew into the side

of the protesters.

The reporter—now taking cover behind his news van—kept on going. "It seems a powered
individual has attacked the marchers and is... Oh my... Don't—"

The camera fell, and a pair of red boots walked into the shot. The camera jostled, then raised. Whoever it was had the red gem in their chest, over the heart.

The camera angled up to see their face. "People of Earth. I've always wanted to say that. I am your new master, Imperius Rex. You will bow down to me." He held out his hand, and a flash of red
ended the signal.

For an instant, Eddie could have sworn it was Zealot back from the dead. But the face wasn't
his. It belonged to someone else.

Blair and Eddie looked at each other in amazement. "Lester?"

The End.

About Author

As a young boy, Stephen Hudler read lots of comic books and wanted to be a superhero. After realizing that wasn't a valid career choice, he opted to just read the comics. Many years later, he got married, started a family and worked hard to provide a good life for them, yet in the back of his mind he still thought about that young boy and his desire to be a superhero. Knowing that was something that could never happen in real life, Stephen did the next best thing. He wrote a book about them, Deadlock.

Stephen lives in the Outer Banks of North Carolina with his wife, Amy, their daughter and rescue cat. When he's not working on his next book, Stephen likes to flip through the comics at his local comic shop, grill tasty foods for family and friends and watch classic episodes of Doctor Who.

You can follow him on:
Blog: stephenhudler.com
YouTube: https://www.youtube.com/c/TheNERDWay1
Facebook and Instagram: @stephenhudler

Made in the USA
Las Vegas, NV
06 October 2025

29195824R00114